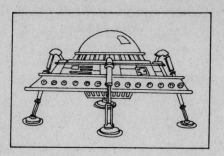

C.O.L.A.R.

Other Avon Camelot Books by
Alfred Slote

MY ROBOT BUDDY
MY TRIP TO ALPHA 1

ALFRED SLOTE is well known for his sports fiction and, more recently, his science fiction. He has written many books for adults and children and his novel JAKE was an ABC-TV After School Special called RAGTAG CHAMPS. Mr. Slote lives in Ann Arbor, Michigan.

C.O.L.A.R.

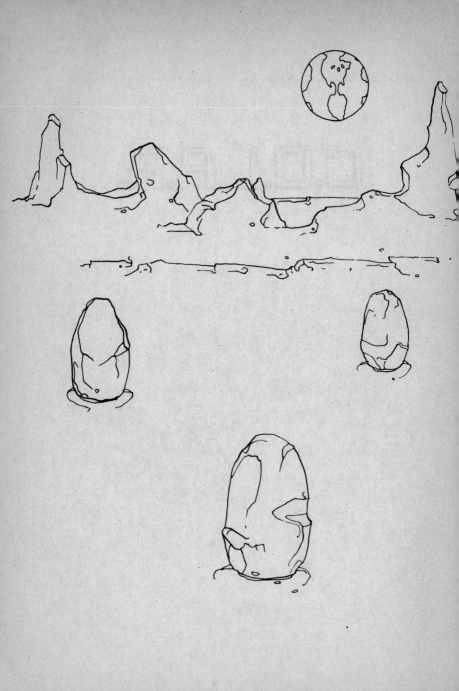

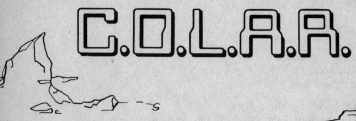

C.O.L.A.R.

A Tale of Outer Space

Alfred Slote

Illustrated by Anthony Kramer

AN AVON CAMELOT BOOK

To Carol Orlin

5th grade reading level has been determined by using the Fry Readability Scale.

AVON BOOKS
A division of
The Hearst Corporation
959 Eighth Avenue
New York, New York 10019

Copyright © 1981 by Alfred Slote
Interior Illustrations Copyright © 1981 by Anthony Kramer
Designed by Kohar Alexanian
Published by arrangement with J.B. Lippincott Junior Books
Library of Congress Catalog Card Number: 80-8723
ISBN: 0-380-63982-3

The J.B. Lippincott edition contains the following Library
of Congress Cataloging in Publication Data:

Slote, Alfred.
  C.O.L.A.R.

  SUMMARY: Stranded on an unknown planet when their
spaceship runs out of fuel, the Jameson family must
rely on their robot to save their lives.
  [1. Robots—Fiction. 2. Science fiction]
I. Kramer, Anthony. II. Title.
PZ7.S635Cad 1981   [E]   80-8723

First Camelot Printing, July, 1983

CAMELOT TRADEMARK REG. U.S. PAT. OFF. AND IN
OTHER COUNTRIES, MARCA REGISTRADA, HECHO EN
U.S.A.

Printed in the U.S.A.

DON 10 9 8 7 6 5 4 3 2 1

CONTENTS

1

EMERGENCY LANDING IN SPACE

"Well, gang," Dad said with that casual tone that I knew meant we were in big trouble, "I'm sorry about this."

He nosed our family spaceship gently into a crater.

"*You're* sorry," Mom said. "I've got a PTA meeting at the school tonight. I'll never get to it now."

"You never know," Dad said, turning up the air valve and reaching for the charts, "the fuel patrol might come along right away."

"Boy, I sure hope not," I whispered to Danny, my robot buddy.

Danny grinned. He knew I wasn't anxious to start school tomorrow. I was going into sixth grade and that is a tough grade. Danny, lucky stiff, doesn't have to go to school. He's a robot.

An Atkins's Robot. He's one of the smartest and most expensive models ever made.

If Danny wants to know something, let's say in arithmetic or history or science, we just send him over to Dr. Atkins's factory and the doctor programs him to know it.

If you read *My Robot Buddy*, in which I told you how we fooled a robotnapper, you know all about me and Danny. He was a birthday present for me on my tenth birthday. He was constructed and designed to look a lot like me. In fact, now that he's lost his freckles we're almost twins. You couldn't tell us apart except when we're walking together. Danny walks stiff-in-the-knees the way robots all over the universe do. However, I can imitate that walk pretty well, and when I do, look out, because you'll never know who's Jack Jameson (me) and who's Danny Jameson (him).

I tell you all this because it can confuse people.

And not only does Danny look a lot like me but he was programmed by Dr. Atkins to *be* just like me. We like to have fun together. We climb trees, go fishing, play ball, and most important, we have adventures.

Running out of fuel halfway between M Colony where we rented a summer home and Earth where we live looked like a real adventure.

"Let's see where we are," Dad said. He had a chart in his lap and he pushed the button for the computer map.

The comp-map is a standard part of every family spaceship. It lines up your route for you. All you have to do, if you've lost your way, is put a chart of our solar system against the comp-map and you can pretty well see where you are.

Most of the time, that is.

This time the comp-map didn't light up—which meant either that it was broken or we were in a part of the solar system that hadn't been charted.

"What do you know about that?" Dad said. "I don't see how we can let the Space Patrol know where we are if we don't know ourselves."

"You should have checked the fuel tank before we left, Frank," Mom said.

"You're right," Dad said, trying not to get mad. When you *know* you've done something stupid, it never helps to have someone tell you too.

So while Dad buried his temper and his nose in his charts, Danny and I climbed to the back of the ship and looked out the rear window.

There wasn't very much to look at.

"Just like the moon," Danny observed.

"Only worse," I said.

Just a couple of weeks ago Danny and I had taken one of those guided Moon Walks you can get for ten dollars—me in my air helmet and Danny just the way he was. Apart from the excitement of being able to jump fifty feet in the moon vacuum, it was a pretty dull walk. I mean: no trees, no grass, no water, no colors . . . nothing but gray craters and gray rocks. This place looked to be the same kind of deal.

"I think," Dad said, "we're in the middle of Asteroid Belt Number Twenty-two."

"Wonderful," Mom said. "And just where is Asteroid Belt Number Twenty-two?"

"Well," Dad said cheerfully, "it's somewhere between M Colony and Earth. And it isn't on the charts because it wasn't here till just a couple of years ago. It was formed by a planet exploding in Omega galaxy, and parts drifted about till they got stuck in Earth's gravity."

"Hey," I said, "if it was a planet that means I can get out and explore a little."

"It means nothing of the sort, Jack. You sit right where you are. By the look of things out there, there's little or no atmosphere. Those craters tell us that."

Earth's thick atmosphere burns up most meteorites so they don't crash and make holes in the land. But lots of space bodies don't have an atmosphere, or else have a pretty thin one, and so meteorites bang into them and make crater holes.

No atmosphere means no air to breathe—okay for Danny who's a robot, but not so okay for me, Jack Jameson, a flesh-and-blood kid.

"What about my air helmet, Dad? I can wear that."

"We don't wear our air helmets unless we have to," Dad said. "They're for emergencies. No one's going anywhere until I find out exactly where we are."

"I could go out there and explore, Dad," Danny said.

"I know you can, Danny," Dad said, "but you're part of this family and we're all going to stick together."

Atkins's Robots, being the best robots in the world, are practically self-contained. They don't need air or water or anything except battery charges from either solar or nuclear batteries. Danny gets a charge every sixteen hours. That's my job at home or up at M Colony—to make sure Danny's batteries are always charged.

M Colony is an orbiting space colony about twenty miles long and five miles wide. It was designed and built by Atkins's Robots years ago when we began running out of space back home. The Atkins's Robots transported dirt and water and grass and horses and cows into this big plastic space station. Inside it they made lakes and rivers and waterfalls; they set the temperature to a nice eighteen degrees Celsius the year round. Pretty soon it was the best place in the solar system to go for summer vacations. According to Dad, who's been around, M Colony has the best trout fishing in our whole galaxy.

This past winter Dad drew a lucky lottery

number and that's how we got our chance to rent up there.

It was kind of odd going up there with Danny, though. You see, there are lots of Atkins's Robots up there, mostly boys and girls, since they cost less to manufacture than adults. The robot boys and girls do most of the work there: garbage disposal, housecleaning, laundry, gardening, painting, street cleaning.

Danny wasn't programmed to do things like that, or to be a servant, the way the others were. So he didn't really feel comfortable making friends with the other robot boys and girls. Of course, he and I hung around together and did lots of neat things so the human boys and girls I met up there kind of resented this.

"I mean, Jameson," a boy said to me one day, "how can you have a robot as a pal? He's not a human being."

"He's more than my pal, friend. He's my brother. He's programmed to look like me and to be like me. He's got emotions, feelings. . . . He's my buddy, my brother."

What more could I say?

But they just didn't understand and they didn't trust Danny. Robots were robots, they felt, and humans were humans and the two weren't supposed to mix. And they believed this because *their* robots were programmed only to work for them. And if their robots ran away (as some robot boys and girls were beginning to do), their work didn't get done and people felt sorry for themselves and got angry at the robots.

The fact was: runaway Atkins's Robots were becoming a big problem at M Colony and on Earth too. One day a whole bunch of boy and girl Atkins's Robots took off in someone's spaceship. (How they got past the Space Police no one will ever know.) Then, too, on homeward trips from M Colony to Earth, families would report that their Atkins's Robots jumped ship, got off somewhere in space. They were never seen again.

Floating around in space sounds crazy and it would kill an air-breathing human being right away. But for a robot, especially an Atkins's Robot, it's no problem.

But Danny Jameson wasn't running away. Any more than I was. We had too much fun together. Although I was beginning to think the spot we were in right now might not be much fun. Outside the spaceship there was just a lot of gray dirt, craters, and rocks. Some of the rocks looked odd. They looked like gravestones that had fallen millions of miles through space and then landed kerplunk! upright in the dirt, and stuck there.

Unless you're a geologist or a rock collector, rocks aren't very interesting. I mean: what can you do with a big rock besides sit on it?

"Jack," Danny whispered.

"What's up?"

"That rock over there. The one closest to us. You see it?"

"Yeah."

"It wasn't that close a minute ago."

"What do you mean?"

"I think it's moving."

"Rocks don't move, Danny. You just think it moved. It—" And then I shut up because right in front of my eyes and Danny's that old gray rock glided a few feet toward us.

I couldn't believe it.

"Hey, I saw it too. That's fantastic!"

"I don't like it," Danny said.

"Why not?"

"Rocks aren't supposed to move."

"Back on Earth maybe. Or up at M Colony. But we don't write the rules for the rest of the universe. I think it's great. I bet we've landed in Rockland."

I said that last word a little too loud. (I was getting excited.) Dad heard it. "Rockland," he repeated. "There's no Rockland on the charts. No, boys, I'm afraid we're lost. I'm going to fiddle with the radio and hope the Space Patrol hears our signal and can home in on us."

"While you're doing that, Dad, is it okay if Danny and I go outside and ask a citizen of this land just where we are?"

"There's no one out there, Jack," Dad said.

"Yes, there is, Dad," Danny said. "Jack and I have been watching a rock walk toward us."

"Oh, my Lord," Mom said. "We must get out of here immediately."

Dad is a sport, though. "This I've got to see," he said, and he scrambled back to join us at the rear window. After a moment Mom came too. You don't see rocks walk every day.

"Which rock is it?" Dad asked.

"The big one there. The one closest to us."

"It doesn't have wheels," Mom said. "I don't see how it can move."

Just then, as though it had heard Mom, and wanted to demonstrate otherwise, that rock glided about three feet closer to our ship.

"What will they think of next!" Mom said.

Dad said: "Of animal, vegetable, and mineral, only animal is supposed to move under its own power."

"How about creeping vines?" I said.

"Plants are powered by the sun," Dad said.

"Well, there's always me," Danny said, with a half grin. "I guess I'm mineral with all my wires, levers, sensors, actuators, silicon chips."

"You're powered by battery charges," I said. "And we're powered by what we eat. And something is powering that rock."

"If it is a rock—," Danny said.

"What do you mean?" Dad asked.

"Maybe it just looks like a rock. Maybe that's what the people who live on this planet look like."

"Danny's got a point," Dad said. "Anyway, I'm going to get my camera. I want to get some tape of this. I'll send it to *Universal Geographic* when we get back."

"You mean *if* we get back," Mom said. "Suppose that rock decides to march right in here?"

Dad had his camera out and was aiming it toward the rock, which was only about thirty feet away from us now. It didn't look like anything but a rock—a few cracks the way rocks often have, but nothing like eyes, ears, nose, or mouth.

"That rock won't be able to get in here, Helen," Dad said, pushing the button. The cassette began to whirr. "The walls of our ship are too thick for that. Come on, Mr. Rock, get moving."

But the rock was now standing still, as though it had heard Dad's order and was trying to prove something to him.

"Hmm—" Dad said, frustrated.

"Maybe he doesn't like to have his picture taken," I suggested.

"Apparently not. I wonder if it's alive in our sense."

"And if it can think," I added.

"It's alive," Danny said quietly, "and it can think, all right."

We looked at him surprised. Atkins's Robots can know lots of things people can't.

"How do you know, Danny?" Dad asked.

"It's trying to talk to me."

"I don't hear anything," Dad said.

"Me neither," I said.

"What's he saying?" Dad asked.

"Nothing yet," Danny said. "But he's giving me a signal. I can hear it. You're going to hear it too . . . in a few seconds."

And hear it we did. It started out as a faint, high-pitched whining noise. Not pleasant at all.

"So that's rock talk," I said. "Rocks sing soprano."

"Shsh, Jack," Dad said. "Danny, can you make any sense out of that noise?"

"No, Dad. It doesn't make any sense to me at all, but I can feel he's trying to tell me something."

Danny's face was very grave. He looked worried.

"It's a dreadful noise and it's getting louder," Mom said.

And so it was. Louder and louder. And more unpleasant every second.

"Frank," Mom said worriedly, "how can those noises come through the thick walls of our ship?"

"I don't know. I was thinking the same

thing," Dad said. And for the first time he looked really worried.

"The noise isn't coming through the walls, Mom," Danny said unhappily. "It's coming through me." He pointed to his belly button behind which was the small radio that every Atkins's Robot is equipped with.

It was true. That was exactly where the awful noise was coming from—out of Danny's belly button.

"Turn it down, Danny," Dad said. "It's starting to hurt my ears."

"I have turned it down," Danny said miserably. "In fact, I've turned it off."

We stared at him because not only was the noise still coming out of his belly button but it was getting louder and louder and more and more painful.

Mom clapped her hands over her ears. I did too. And Dad covered his. But the sound kept coming, like an ocean wave, coming and coming and coming and then covering us with a weight so thick it was impossible to see, hear, to breathe. . . .

Dad understood first what was happening. "He wants to kill us," he shouted.

■ 15

Mom passed out first. She slumped over. I reached for her. When I did that my ears were unprotected and it felt like a ton of water had crashed down on my head. I went down, down, down into the darkness.

My head hit against the window. That was the last thing I felt.

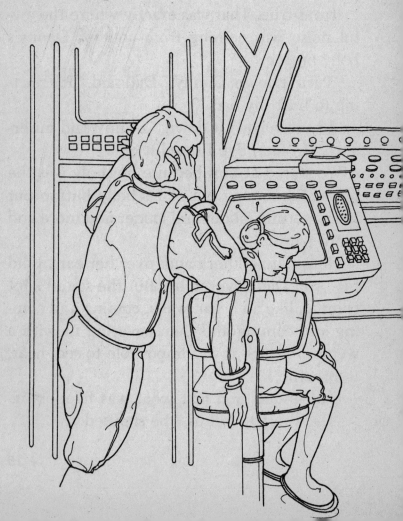

2

DANNY SAVES OUR LIVES

I wasn't dead.

The dead don't dream (I don't think). And I was having a swell dream. In it, Danny and I were back on M Colony climbing trees. He was shinnying up a big oak and I was climbing a maple.

Danny could climb a lot faster than I. Although robots are stiff-in-the-knees, they're strong because they're all steel wires and levers inside their plastic flesh. Secondly, Danny didn't have to carry an emergency air helmet around on his back. Up on M Colony, because the authorities were always worried about a meteorite making a hole in the plastic shield that kept the air inside the colony, humans carried emergency air helmets on their backs.

As I climbed upward, my air helmet bumped

against the back of my head.

So Danny got to the top first and when I got to the top branch of my tree, Danny called out to me: "Isn't it great up here, Jack?"

"Terrific," I yelled back.

We could see for miles around. Kids were playing soccer. Near the soccer fields were robot boys and girls working in vegetable gardens.

There was a small artificial river running downhill to an underground pumping station where the water would be pumped back to repeat its cycle. We could see kids canoeing on the river; other kids were fishing and swimming. Robot boys and girls were working the pumps at the pumping station to make sure the river flowed at its pre-set computer rates. They could manually slow down the river for a fisherman about to land a trout or make it go faster for a canoer who wanted a fast white-water ride.

Overhead was the plastic shield that enveloped M Colony. It was painted sky blue so we would always have a blue sky in the darkness of outer space. And every now and then pretty cloud shapes drifted by. They were projected by gigantic cloud machines. Robots worked the cloud machines, and also the sunset and sunrise machines. Atkins's Robots had also invented rain machines because you could get bored with one beautiful day after another.

M Colony was just like life on Earth without Earth's problems.

"I love it," I shouted from my tree top to Danny, but then suddenly Danny wasn't there. That's how dreams go. Things change without warning. His tree was empty. And then below me I could hear a whining noise. I looked down. To my horror, there at the base of my tree was a strange robot boy. He had a big chain saw in his hands and he was attacking my tree, cutting it down.

"Hey," I yelled down, "don't do that. Do you want to kill me? Stop that right now!"

"It's all right, Jack," Dad said. "It has stopped. The noise has stopped."

I opened my eyes. I wasn't in a tree at M Colony. I was in our family spaceship. And then I remembered the rock that had been trying to kill us with its noise. But everything was silent and peaceful now.

Mom was all right too. She was looking at me anxiously.

"I'm okay," I reassured her. I looked around for Danny. He wasn't there. "Where's Danny?"

Dad hesitated, and then he pointed out the window. I sat up and looked. Danny was there, outside the ship, standing on the surface of this strange planet, talking to the rock.

"Danny saved our lives by jumping out of the ship and taking the noise with him," Dad said.

"Is he going to be all right out there?"

"I think so. Danny is an Atkins's Robot. A very smart robot."

"But suppose the rock attacks him?"

"I don't think it will."

"Dad, we've got to make sure that rock knows that Danny is a part of this family."

It's funny how fast you can accept the idea that a rock is something you can talk to, reason with.

"How do you propose to do that, Jack?"

That was a good question. How do you talk to a rock? How was Danny doing it? Secondly, how could we even worry the rock? Or scare it? We don't carry weapons in our spaceship. Up at M Colony only the Space Police have laser rifles. Ordinary citizens aren't permitted to have guns. And what good would a laser rifle do against a rock anyway?

One glance at Dad told me he had considered all these things too.

"Jack, let's just sit tight for a while and see what happens. Danny knows things we can't possibly know and he can do things we can't do. You can't go out there anyway. The only things that could survive on this unfriendly looking planet are probably rocks and robots. We've got to hold on to our air helmets in case we really need them."

He was right, of course. But still it was hard to sit there and watch your robot brother talk to a rock, maybe argue, and not know what was going on.

I guessed they were arguing because every once in a while Danny would gesture back toward us.

Finally Danny must have won because the rock began to retreat . . . moving backward (without turning around) to where the other rocks stood watching.

We cheered. Mom, Dad, and me. A victory for our side!

But our cheers were short-lived. Instead of coming back to the ship, Danny walked after the rock, following it, as though he were drawn by a magnet. He walked with that stiff-in-the-knees gait that I have so much fun imitating.

"Now what?" I said.

"Frank," Mom said, "call Danny back."

"How?" Dad asked helplessly.

Danny's shoes sank into the powdery dust of the surface so it looked almost as though he too were gliding. Maybe the rock had feet we couldn't see because of the dust.

"I don't like this, Frank."

"I don't either, Helen. But what can I do about it?"

"Dad, let me go out there and stand by Danny so they'll know he's not alone."

"That might make it worse, Jack. They might take Danny hostage if they know there are more of us."

"And you too," Mom said.

"They've stopped walking," Dad said.

The big rock stopped when it got back to where the other rocks were.

Now Danny stood there in front of all the rocks, pleading his case. *Our* case. I knew he was talking to them because he kept fingering his belly button. He was talking to them over his radio.

Then Danny walked around the rock. The rock was a little bigger than he was, so we lost sight of him. We waited for him to reappear on the other side. But he didn't.

"Now what's going on?" Dad asked.

"I'm going out there," I said.

"Wait!"

"My God," Mom said.

None of us could believe what we were seeing. All the rocks . . . there were five of them in that particular cluster, began slowly sinking into the ground. Down . . . down . . . down they sank, and slowly disappeared below the surface, until all of a sudden there was nothing left but the same dull, gray dust that was everywhere on this planet.

Danny was gone too!

That was too much for me.

Although Dad was holding on to my arm, I broke his grip. I ran for the doors.

"Jack!" Dad yelled.

But I wasn't listening anymore. I'd listened to him too long. I'd stayed in the ship too long. I should have followed my instincts and gone out sooner to help Danny. Maybe now it was too late, but I'd find out.

I burst through the inner air lock and then out the outer air lock with Dad yelling something at me. But I couldn't hear him. I didn't want to hear him. I wanted to get out there as fast as possible.

I jumped five feet down from our spaceship onto the strange land. It was only when my shoes sank into the gray powdery dust and the cold white stars were twinkling in the black sky over my head that I realized I didn't have my air helmet on.

I had jumped into an airless vacuum.

I pitched forward, nose first, into the dust of our large crater.

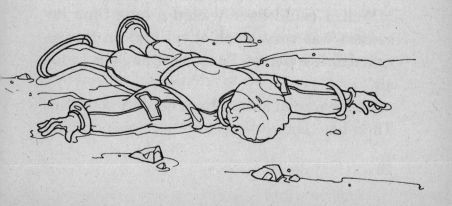

3

ALIVE ON A DEAD PLANET

Air is everything. It's what makes us humans; it's what makes dogs dogs, cats cats; it lets plants live and fish too, because they take in oxygen through their gills.

We're all creatures of air. And when there is no air, we die quickly.

I lay there in our crater, my nose in the dust, and this time I was positive I was dead. I wasn't just knocked unconscious this time; I was certain I was dead. I wasn't dreaming. What I was really doing was waiting to be dead.

Well, I could have waited a long time because I was very much alive. And on this so-called airless planet, I was breathing very good air.

There was an atmosphere here. A good one! Then how come there were all these craters?

I studied the land under my nose and then I sat up and studied the edges of the crater that our ship had landed in. Hmmm . . . I was beginning to see some interesting things. It was not your run-of-the-mill crater. There was definitely something odd about it.

I looked up. The door to the outer air lock of our spaceship opened and the automatic landing ladder came down. Down it climbed Dad and then Mom. They were wearing their air helmets.

I sat up and grinned at them. "You can take those air helmets off. There's as much air here as there is on Earth."

Dad's voice came back to me muffled through his speaker. "Are you sure?"

"Positive. I'm breathing well."

He took off his air helmet. Mom took off hers. They stood there in the bright starlight looking around.

"I don't understand this at all," Dad said. "The surface of this planet is pitted with crater holes. There's no vegetation around. No trees, no bushes, nothing—"

"Dad, this crater was made by people. Look at its edges. They were dug with a shovel. You can see the shovel marks."

Dad squatted down. "You're absolutely right. But why?"

"I'm not sure."

But it was pretty clear that someone wanted to fool us. They had taken the surface of this planet and disguised it to look barren, airless, unfriendly—a place no one would want to land on, unless they strayed off course and ran out of fuel and had nowhere else to land.

"Well," Dad said, "this puts a different light on the matter. Let's get back inside the ship and talk it over."

"Nope. I'm going to find Danny first. He's somewhere under the surface here."

"Jack, be reasonable. Let's keep sending out signals to the Space Patrol. This is something we can't handle alone. If we keep signaling they'll pick us up and locate us with a direction finder."

"While you're doing that, Dad, I'm going to find Danny."

"Jack," Mom said, "why won't you ever listen to your father? The Space Patrol will find us and they'll find Danny too."

"He could be in trouble, Mom. Look, if it

was the other way around, I know that Danny would stick by me. It *was* the other way around a few minutes ago and he saved our lives by jumping out. Now we've got to help him."

"He may not need help," Dad said.

"Let me find that out. Whoever dug these holes are intelligent creatures. We saw Danny talking to them. If he can talk to them, so can I."

"What are you going to say?"

"I want my robot brother back."

"Suppose they won't give him up?"

"I'll take him back."

"How?"

"I don't know yet."

"Suppose they take you too?"

"Then we'll escape together. Aw, Dad—"

There are always a million reasons *not* to do something scary. But sometimes you just have to go ahead and do it. This was one of those times.

Dad didn't see it that way. (Fathers hardly ever do.)

"Jack, I forbid you to leave the ship," he said.

"I've left it already."

"All right, I forbid you to look for Danny."

I love my father. I really do. He's a swell guy. And maybe if I ever become a father I won't let my kids do dangerous things, but I'm not a father yet. Thank goodness.

I walked away from them and over to the spot where the rocks had disappeared into the ground.

My folks came after me, as I knew they would. They knew we had to find Danny. He may be a robot but he's also part of our family.

A little wind was blowing dust up around our ankles. Overhead the stars shone brightly, lighting up the surface. There were no marks in the dust to indicate where the rocks had gone down . . . no marks to indicate where Danny and the rock had even walked. The wind had blown gray dust over everything.

"We better get back to the ship, dear," Mom said to me. "Someone might come up and try to take off in it."

"It has no fuel in it, Helen," Dad said. And when he said that I knew that he too wanted to find Danny really badly.

"Frank, we've seen rocks that walk and talk. Anything can happen in this Godforsaken place. I say we return to the ship."

Dad shook his head. "Jack was right, Helen. Danny left the ship to save us; we've got to try to save him. I think this is about the spot where those rocks went down, don't you, Jack."

"Somewhere around here."

"Well, let's start investigating."

Dad got down on his hands and knees and so did I. After a moment Mom did too.

The problem was we hadn't the slightest idea what we were looking for. An opening? A door? A hole?

We kept sifting through the gray dust, brushing it aside.

We seemed to be getting nowhere until my right hand hit something hard. Metallic.

"Hey, I've found something."

Quickly I brushed the dust away. There below my hand was a metal cover about two feet in diameter, like a small manhole cover you still sometimes see in some of the older cities on Earth.

"What do you think that is?" Mom asked.

"I don't know, but I bet there are more of these about," I replied.

There were. Mom and Dad started brushing furiously and in a few moments we uncovered five more little metal covers in that area.

"Well," Mom said, beaming, "that explains the mystery. Now we can go back to the ship."

"Come on, Mom. This is just the start. We've got to get these covers off and see what's down there. Right, Dad?"

"Right, son."

But that was easier said than done. I couldn't get a grip. The cover was sealed tight. I needed a screwdriver or a knife. Dad didn't have either. He searched in his pockets. He came up with a little pencil flashlight.

"Let me have it."

"It has no sharp edge to it."

"It's getting very cold here," Mom said. "You're both going to get pneumonia."

The wind was whipping up. There was nothing to stop it—no trees, no bushes, no hills . . .

I shone the flashlight on the cover. And that was when, for the first time, I saw the initials: C.O.L.A.R.

"What does it say?" Dad asked.

"Color."

"No, it doesn't." Dad squatted down alongside me. "It says C.O.L.A.R. Those are periods after each letter. These people can read and write."

"That still doesn't tell us how to open the cover. I'm sure the Space Patrol people know all about this place." Mom looked right at me. "I'm certain those rocks can't hurt Danny. He's probably happy and having a good time now."

She wouldn't give up. I guess it's a motherly instinct about trouble.

I ignored her. So did Dad. I ran my finger absently over the C. and the O. and L. and the A. and the R. And then it happened, when my finger touched the period after the R. That "period" wasn't solid the way the other "periods" had been. It gave way under the pressure of my finger.

Like a button.

It was a button.

We all heard something happening below. A noise was coming toward us.

We stepped back, away from the cover. Something was going to happen. . . .

Slowly the cover rose up, pushed up by something gray and big . . . the rock.

"Frank," Mom whispered, "I'm frightened."

"So am I," Dad said. "But let's not show him that. I'll do the talking, Jack."

Dad cleared his throat. "See here," he said loudly, "our name is Jameson. We're from Metro City Seven on Earth. That's in the state of New Jersey. We were on our way back there from a summer vacation in M Colony when we ran out of fuel. We had to make an emergency landing here. We want to be on our way home as soon as possible. But it seems that you, or someone who looks just like you, have taken one of our family. I'm referring to our son Danny Jameson. He's a robot but he's part of our family and we would like him back."

We waited. There was no answer from the rock.

"Look here," Dad said. He took a step closer to the rock. "I mean this. I want my son Danny Jameson returned."

Still the rock was silent . . . no whining noise, no movement—nothing.

"I don't think he hears you," Mom said nervously.

Dad stepped right up against the rock.

"See here, my stony friend. You've got someone from my family with you and I want him returned immediately."

And then for emphasis Dad poked his index finger against the rock.

"Huh?" he said.

The rock surface gave way.

"What is it?" Mom and I said.

"For Pete's sake . . . this isn't a rock at all. It's a fake. See for yourself where my finger went in . . . and almost went through."

Dad's finger had almost made a hole in this so-called rock. I touched the rock. It was soft. Brittle. It was plastic.

"I'll be darned."

"I think we've been tricked," Dad said.

He walked around to the back of the rock. "Look at this, Jack."

Mom and I went around to the other side. The back of the rock wasn't at all like the front. From here you could see it wasn't a rock at all but was actually a little portable house that someone my size, or Danny's, could fit into.

There was a handle that Dad pulled on and a little door swung open. We peered inside but could see nothing.

I gave the flashlight to Dad to shine inside but still we couldn't see anything . . . just a gaping hole, and what looked to be a kind of steel cable.

Dad was awed. "You know what this is? It's an elevator that can become a mobile unit. The elevator comes up, pushing the metal cover in the air which becomes part of the rock. Then someone inside can unhook the unit from the cable and push it along while hiding inside and looking to a stranger in a spaceship just like a walking rock. And then the operator can walk it back to where we are now, right over the hole, hook it up, push some kind of button, and down he goes. And I guess two little people could get inside it."

"That means the people who live here must live undergound."

"It would seem that way."

"But why?"

"I don't know."

"Whoever they are," Mom said, "they're obviously very, very smart."

"That's true."

"Dad, I'm going to go down in that elevator or whatever it is."

"I don't know about that, Jack. We haven't the slightest idea where this thing will take you."

"It's got to take me to Danny."

"Maybe it will, maybe it won't."

"How will you get back?" Mom asked.

"If I can take it down, I can take it up. And Danny will be with me. I promise you that."

I sounded so sure of myself, but I didn't really feel that sure.

"Jack, I don't know. I don't like it," Dad said.

"I promise I'll be careful. That elevator really isn't big enough for you. Besides someone has to stay here and keep signaling the Space Patrol. You and Mom look after each other. I'll be all right. I know I will."

Mom and Dad looked at each other.

"No," Mom said.

"I don't think we have a choice if we want to find Danny," Dad said slowly. "Jack, promise me you won't take any chances."

"I promise."

"Use your head about things. Try to think like Danny does."

"I will."

Little did I know what a good piece of advice this would be.

"And if you get in trouble . . . come right back up."

"I will. Don't worry. I'm going to make it and make it back with Danny."

"What time do you have, Jack?"

"Why?"

"Because I'm going to give you an hour. If you're not back in an hour, I'm going to wedge myself into another one of these things and go down after you."

I checked the time. It was 4:00 A.M. Dad and I synchronized our watches.

"One hour, Jack."

"Okay, Dad. One hour."

"Jack!" Mom held out her arms. I went and gave her a quick hug and then gave Dad a quick hug too.

Then I stepped inside the so-called rock. A small platform, a skirt really, ran around its bottom. You were obviously supposed to put your feet on it. Otherwise you'd fall right down the center of the elevator shaft. Once settled, I shut the door. Through cracks in the rock, I could see our spaceship. I could also see Mom and Dad looking anxious. Now I knew why the rock had walked backward away from the ship—so we wouldn't see the door. It was all beginning to make sense.

But what kind of people had robotnapped Danny? And why? They had to be small to fit inside rocks like these.

That, somehow, was a little reassuring.

I stood inside the rock and waited for it to go down. But it didn't.

"Look for a button," Dad said.

I ran my fingers around the inside of the rock. And then I felt it off to my right—a button not set into the plastic, but set into something firm like wood or metal. A wire must run down from it.

Here goes nothing, I thought.

I pushed the button.

And down I went.

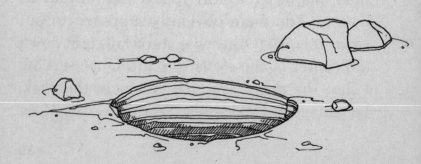

"WHAT ARE YOU DOING HERE?"

Back home in Metro City Seven, New Jersey, there are all kinds of elevators. Super expresses, expresses, locals, freight—fast freight and slow. There are elevators that take you to interplanetary rocket stations, that take you to the terminals for intercontinental space shuttles. There are elevators inside our school that take you up to the roof pad for those kids who come to school by solar air bus.

So elevators are nothing new to me. I don't like them, though. Fast elevators give me a funny feeling in my stomach when they slow down, and slow elevators are just plain boring.

This "rock" elevator was absolutely the slowest I'd ever been on. It was *so* slow, some of the time I wasn't even sure it was moving. To check, twice during the trip down I opened the door. It didn't open very far before it banged into a dirt wall. I hoped whoever lived inside this planet (they sure didn't live *on* it) had stairways in case they had to get to the surface in a hurry.

Finally the elevator hit bottom. The whirring noise stopped.

I opened the door a crack and peered out. Nothing.

I opened it all the way and stepped into a large room with ceiling, floor, and walls—but absolutely nothing in it. I noticed another elevator next to mine, and then three more. Five rocks in that cluster on the surface equalled five elevators. Everything made some kind of sense, though I didn't understand exactly what.

But now what do I do?

Dad says: when in doubt, do nothing.

So for a few minutes I did nothing. But nothing's hard work when you're in a hurry. I decided to explore the room. There was a door to my left and a door to my right.

Something was printed on the door to my right. I went over and examined it.

It said: WELCOME TO C.O.L.A.R.

Those darn initials again. What could they stand for? Committee? Country? Congress?

There was only one way to find out and that was to open the door and step into C.O.L.A.R., whatever that was.

I was about to do just that when I heard voices. They were coming from behind me. Quickly I flattened myself against a side wall and prayed that I could not be spotted.

The other door opened and into the room came two boys . . . about my age. Only I saw right away they weren't real boys. They were robot boys. They walked stiff-in-the-knees and they were talking to each other.

One had blond hair, the other brown.

The one with the blond hair said: "I'm very excited."

The other one said: "So am I. We haven't had an escapee for a while."

"I'm not sure he's an escapee. Carl Three told me he jumped out of his master's ship in order to save him."

"How horrible. A brainwashed robot."

"Jeff will certainly work on that."

The blond one opened the door I'd been looking at and they went through it.

I thought about what they'd said. They had to be talking about Danny. But calling him an "escapee"? What was this place all about? Was this a land of robots? And what did C.O.L.A.R. stand for?

I went back to the door and stared at those initials as though they could start talking to me and explaining themselves. I was a little scared to open the door. Suppose it locked and I couldn't get back? Well, you've got to do something, Jack Jameson! You're not going to find Danny standing here and worrying.

And then, without warning, the door behind me opened again. I spun around. A girl was standing there. She had blond hair and a nice face. She looked at me puzzled.

"What are you doing here?" she asked.

I kept my face blank. She thinks she knows me. She thinks she's met me. I've never seen her before in my life. Best to stall . . .

"I . . . uh—"

She walked stiff-in-the-knees up to me.

"Don't you remember me?" she said. "I'm Ann Two and you, Danny Seven, are supposed to be in the reprogramming room. That's where Carl Three and I left you. Jeff wanted you completely reprogrammed. He's very worried about you."

Danny Seven, I thought. They've changed his name.

"Well, Ann Two," I quickly thought to say, "I finished with the reprogramming and decided to walk around a bit."

She shook her head. She wasn't angry with me. "Danny Seven, you couldn't have finished that quickly. Your input wires must have come loose. No one likes being reprogrammed but some of us just have to be. And you had the worst case of humanitis we've seen in a long time."

Humanitis? What kind of disease was that?

"Come along now," she said. "I'm going to take you back to reprogramming."

Ann Two opened the door I had been staring at. I had no choice now. I had to follow her in. And I did, taking care to walk stiff-in-the-knees.

The door clicked shut behind me.

I was finally inside C.O.L.A.R. Whatever that was.

Strange New World
Underground

Later people would ask me: "What was it like, Jack?" How could a bunch of Atkins's Robots, intelligent and energetic as they are, build a whole new world below the surface of a planet?

The answer is: I don't know how they did it. It really wasn't a very beautiful world. It wasn't the world we were given for nothing on Earth, the world of sun and light, rain and snow, trees and brooks. It was a world they *had* to create. And they did it. And it was theirs.

Ann Two led me through a series of rooms and when she realized I was staring open-mouthed at everything, she remembered (thank goodness!) that I hadn't been given a tour when I first came down.

"We were in a terrible hurry to have you reprogrammed. Well, I'll give you a quick tour right now."

We were passing through a series of large underground rooms, each one very different from the other, connected by small passageways.

The first room we came to looked very familiar. It was a gym with basketball hoops at either end. What was unfamiliar were robots playing basketball. Three boys and three girls were playing at one basket. It wasn't boys against girls; one team had two girls, the other had two boys. They all played at the same level of ability—not very good. I'd never seen robots play basketball before. On Earth or up at M Colony robots just don't play games. Except for Danny.

These robots were having a lot of fun. They were calling out to one another, even those on the other team:

"Good shot, Fred Two."

"Well played, Marnie Four."

"I believe it's my turn to shoot, Sam Six."

I almost laughed out loud at their politeness. It was just the opposite of how we humans played. We were always yelling at each other, trying to rattle our opponent, take advantage and get him or her off balance. These players were actually cheering one another on.

Ann Two, watching me, smiled. "I know what you're thinking, Danny Seven. You're wondering when was the last time you saw robots play anything, not just basketball. Well, here in C.O.L.A.R. we play all the games that human beings won't let us play on Earth."

But on Earth, I thought, Danny and I played basketball together all the time.

Careful, Jack, I said to myself, you're Danny from now on. Danny Seven, at that.

I said to her: "I played basketball back on Earth."

Her smile disappeared. "You obviously did not finish your reprogramming or you wouldn't be saying something like that. You're still brainwashed. Come along, Danny Seven. I've got to get you back to reprogramming immediately!"

From the noisy but polite gym, we stepped into a room that was absolutely silent. About a dozen robot boys and girls sat around watching Vue/Screens. They wore earphones so that the sound wouldn't bother anyone who wanted to read.

There were quite a few robots reading books. Where had they got the books? Where were they getting Vue/Screen programs from? I couldn't quite believe what I was seeing. It looked like a media center in school back home, but quieter.

"Where do you get your Vue/Screen programs from?" I asked her.

"From Earth and M Colony. We have a receiver up on the surface disguised as a rock. Someday Jeff says we'll have our own programs, our own studios, and instead of watching shows in which human beings are the heroes, we'll have programs in which robots are heroes."

I'd never thought of that before. Back home I'd never seen a Vue/Screen program in which a robot was a hero. Robots were just human-looking machines people bought to do their work. Except, of course, for Danny, who was different.

"Would you really like to live the way human beings do?" I asked Ann Two.

It was a dangerous question to have asked.

"Wouldn't you?" she snapped. And then she relaxed. "I forgot. You've been programmed by Dr. Atkins to believe you're as good as a human being. You've also been programmed to believe you were having fun with your master. Well, you're just going to need more reprogramming input than Jeff thought, more than any of us thought, for that matter. Come along!"

From the media center-library, we walked through a passageway and then into an entirely different kind of room. Here robot boys and girls sat around playing music. They had instruments that looked like guitars. When we entered, a boy was singing while the others accompanied him.

This was what he was singing:

> *I'm a robot*
> *Lost in space;*
> *I'm a robot*
> *With a human face.*
>
> *But then I followed*
> *A distant star;*
> *Now I'm free*
> *In C.O.L.A.R.*

And then the others joined in the chorus:

Now he's free
In C.O.L.A.R.

Ann Two turned to me. "How do you like that song?"

"It's nice." I took a deep breath. Now was the opportunity. I just hoped they hadn't already told Danny the answer to this.

"I forget," I said. "What does C.O.L.A.R. stand for, Ann Two?"

She regarded me curiously. "You didn't forget, Danny Seven. No one's told you. You'll be told when you become an official citizen here."

"Oh—"

"You really are one confused little robot. You should never have left reprogramming. Do you see what confusion and trouble you're causing for yourself? Come along."

Before we left, the robot boy who had been singing called out to us. "Hey, Ann Two, ask Danny Seven if he'd like to join our music group."

"Later," Ann Two said. "I'm sure he'll want

to learn to play a musical instrument."

"Oh," I said, as we walked through a passageway, "I can play the piano."

"Stop talking that way," Ann Two said. "You're making me think you're crazy and not just brainwashed."

They'd never understand, I thought, how Danny is really family. When I was given piano lessons during the winter, so was Danny.

Ann Two went on: "Human beings don't spend money to give robots piano lessons. You've got to stop that kind of talk."

I did.

From the passageway off the music room, we entered a small room with chairs and tables. Robot boys and girls were playing games that looked like chess and checkers. They also played electronic games on Vue/Screens.

They were so engrossed that not one of them looked up at us.

"Doesn't anyone work here?" I asked.

She looked relieved at my question. "That's better. That's normal. Now you sound more like a robot. No, Danny Seven, that's the whole idea of C.O.L.A.R. We don't have to work here.

Here we play the way human beings do. Although there is one room where work goes on. And you will be expected to work three hours a week there."

"What's that?" I asked, hoping I wasn't supposed to know.

"C.O.L.A.R. Control. We'll be there in a moment. But first, here's our dancing room—"

She needn't have told me that. The moment we entered I could see that this waxed and shining room was given over entirely to dancing. Music was coming out of a loudspeaker and robot boys and girls were jumping up and down, laughing. They were not very graceful, but they seemed to be having fun. Several of them waved at us. Ann Two waved back. I did too. I was beginning to get a kick out of pretending to be Danny, but at the same time, a small worrisome thought was beginning to grow inside me. Dad had given me an hour to find Danny and bring him back.

I sneaked a look at my watch. I'd used up about fifteen minutes. Forty-five minutes to go.

Have to hurry. Dad would be in big trouble

down here. It was a land of kids . . . robot kids, to be sure, but kids. He'd stick out like a sore thumb. He couldn't pretend to be anything other than he was—a human being.

And they hated human beings here.

Ann Two was looking at me. She was obviously waiting for me to make some comment about how I danced on Earth.

"No," I said truthfully, "I'm no good at dancing."

"No robot is," she said, "but the point is that here in C.O.L.A.R. we can do things we're no good at. Human beings are afraid to do that on Earth. They're always worried about making fools of themselves. Here we have fun, and that is what we are learning to be good at. Having fun."

I looked at her. "Why are you doing the same things down here that humans do?"

The question surprised her. She thought about it a moment. Then she smiled. "You're a smart robot," she said. "The answer is: unfortunately, we want to be like humans. We've been created in their image, and we have no other image. It's awful. I don't like it. But I'm part of it too. . . . This next room, for instance—"

She opened the door and I followed her inside and gasped.

This was the most unusual of all the rooms. At first I wasn't even sure it was a room—it was so big. The ceiling, way up high, was a blue sky and there was sunlight and a cloud drifting across. On the ground—there was no floor here—there was earth and grass and a brook and trees and some bushes. Robot boys and girls were seated by the brook talking; one boy was fishing off a little bridge.

"Why, this is beautiful. Why on earth would you hate it?"

"Because it's not *on Earth*. Because it's not real," she said bitterly. "Because it only reminds me that we're not able to live on the surface the way human beings do. Here in the Earthroom we imitate Earth, but the grass is plastic, the clouds are chemical, the sunlight is electronic, the brook is recycled by pumps, and I hate it. I'd give anything to plant a real tree, touch a real tree, watch a real tree grow, climb it when it's full grown. But that can only happen on the surface and we can't live on the surface."

"Why not?"

"Jeff explained that to you, Danny Seven. I was there when he did. Stop playing games with me. Come along, we're almost there."

The answer to that would have to wait.

The next room we went into was strangely familiar. It was C.O.L.A.R. Control, and I knew where I had seen its prototype back on Earth: Dr. Atkins's robot factory—where he had robots building robots and robots giving emergency battery charges to robots all over the world!

This room was a hive of activity. There were computers, terminals, solar and nuclear power packs, generators, communication consoles.

Architecturally, C.O.L.A.R. Control consisted of a winding circular ramp lined with banks of electronic instruments. Robot boys and girls stood there working them, fiddling with dials, pushing buttons, watching red, white, and blue lights blink on and off, as energy levels of robots flashed in front of them.

There was a main terminal in the center of the room. Seated at it was a tall, slender

boy. He was watching the progress of an emergency battery charge being given to a robot somewhere in C.O.L.A.R.

We waited till he was satisfied that everything was okay, then Ann Two said: "Jeff, I found Danny Seven wandering around near the elevators."

Jeff turned. I found myself looking into a pair of very intelligent, piercing blue eyes. They reminded me of someone else . . . and then I knew who: Dr. Atkins . . . he had those same cool, inquisitive blue eyes.

This wasn't surprising. I learned later that Jeff had belonged to Dr. Atkins himself. Jeff had been one of the designers of M Colony. He was programmed to know just about everything, to be tough and hard and unyielding.

Those blue eyes bore into me. Did he know my secret? Could he tell I wasn't a robot?

"Bring him here," Jeff said.

6

A SCARY MOMENT

"No one," Jeff said cold , "eve leaves reprogramming until I detacn their neuro-wires. How did you get out?"

To be a good liar you have to really believe you're telling the truth—for the moment.

I looked Jeff right in the eye. "They came loose," I said. "I don't know how it happened. I figured you ended reprogramming that way. When my input was enough, the wires came loose. So I just walked out."

"And then where did you go?"

"I wandered around."

That seemed to be the safest answer to that.

"He must have gone the back way through the tunnels, Jeff," a robot boy, who had been listening to us, said.

"Get me his computer program, Carl Three."

Carl Three went over to a stack of paper. He moved quickly, for a robot. There was no doubt who ran this place.

Jeff's eyes never left mine. He doesn't quite believe me, I thought. I stared back at him with a frank and open face.

"I want to see how far you were in the reprogramming before you walked out," he said.

"I don't think he got very far," Ann Two said. "He's been saying some very crazy things to me—that he played the piano on Earth, that he played basketball. I think I better return him to reprogramming, Jeff, and you can hook him right up again."

"We'll make sure where he was when he walked out," Jeff said. "Thanks, Carl Three."

Carl Three handed Jeff some computer printout. Jeff studied it. Then he looked up at me.

"All right, Danny Seven, I'm going to ask you some questions."

"Fire away," I said cockily. I was really doing pretty good so far.

"What's your name?"

"Danny Jameson."

"Wrong!" he snapped. "Your name is Danny Seven! You were being reprogrammed to be Danny Seven! There are six other Dannies here. Repeat: Danny Seven. I am Danny Seven."

"Danny Seven. I am Danny Seven."

"What do you think of human beings, Danny Seven?"

I glanced at Ann Two. I could see now where all this was leading. But I couldn't fake it with Jeff after telling Ann Two that I liked human beings, they were nice to me, that I had played basketball and had had piano lessons and all that.

"I really like my family on Earth. They treat me like one of them. I am one of them."

"Obviously the reprogramming didn't take at all, Jeff," Carl Three said.

Jeff's cold blue eyes were angry. "You ripped your neuro-wires off in the very beginning. You're a foolish, stubborn robot, Danny Seven. If this happens again I'm going to break you down for parts. All right, Ann Two, take him back there. As soon as I finish monitoring these charges, I'll be along. And I'll make sure your neuro-wires are firmly attached this time."

Ann Two looked concerned. "Jeff," she said, "if the robot doesn't want to live in C.O.L.A.R., why must we make him?"

I leaned forward to hear the answer. This was a big question.

"Come on, Ann Two," Jeff replied, "no one who comes to C.O.L.A.R. can leave. You know that as well as I do. If we let him go, the Space Patrol will get hold of him and find out just where we are and how we live. We spend a lot of time disguising this planet so it looks uninhabitable. We're not going to let a robot out any more than I'm going to allow the human family in the spaceship to go free. As soon as Danny Seven is completely reprogrammed and he understands what the truth really is, he's going to go back up to his master's spaceship. They'll let him in and we will finish off what we started before: sound beaming them to death.

"Now, take him away. I'll be along in a few minutes to finish his reprogramming."

Ann Two sighed. "Come along, Danny Seven."

I went with her . . . gladly.

7

ANN TWO'S STORY

Ann Two was silent as we left C.O.L.A.R. Control.

"I've never seen Jeff get so angry," she finally said.

"I don't think he's very nice," I said.

"He works very hard. He's the only citizen of C.O.L.A.R. who works all the time. He has a terrible responsibility. C.O.L.A.R. was his idea, he designed it, built it, and anyone who is a threat to it is his enemy."

"I'm not a threat to it," I said.

I meant that too, not only in *my* disguise as Danny, but in my real feelings as Jack Jameson. You had to admire what these robots had constructed down here below the surface of the planet.

"You could be," she said. "You could be a

spy from Dr. Atkins. For a robot, you've certainly behaved oddly—first wanting to save your master—"

"I'm telling you, they're family."

She sighed. "Let's not start that again. Secondly, ripping your neuro-wires off. Did you really do that, Danny Seven?"

"Yes," I lied.

"Why?"

"Because I'm not really brainwashed, Ann Two. I'm really part of a human family. I love them. And they love me. I was programmed to be a brother to a human boy named Jack Jameson."

"What is he like, Danny Seven?"

"He's nice—" It was funny talking this way about myself. I'm glad my folks weren't hearing this: "He's a nice kid. Of course, he's not perfect. He does dumb things and says dumb things, but he does his own chores, he makes his own bed, he mows the lawn. I don't do his work for him. We're brothers and buddies, and I was programmed to have fun with him."

"I don't believe you."

"You think I'm lying."

"I think you've been brainwashed."

"How can I convince you otherwise?"

"Where is your so-called brother-buddy now?" she asked. "Is he worried about you? No, far from it. He's probably sitting up in that spaceship calling the Space Patrol to come rescue him and his family. You don't see him looking for you right now, even though you saved his life . . . do you?"

Boy, what I wouldn't have given to be able to tell her the truth. But the truth would be dangerous right now.

I was silent. And she took my silence for agreement.

"Danny Seven, you'll be happier when you've been reprogrammed. It's not normal for robots to like humans and for humans to be nice to robots. I know that from my own experience—"

She hesitated. We were walking through a long, narrow passageway.

"What was your master like, Ann Two?

"Awful," she said. "It was a human family with a mother, father, two daughters and a son. They bought me from Dr. Atkins and had me programmed to cook, clean, do laundry, help the children with their homework, mow the lawn in summer, shovel snow in winter, mop, dust, go shopping for them. I hated it. They had me programmed to be smart enough to help their kids get through school, but that meant I was also smart enough to want a better life than a slave's."

"And you've found that better life here?"

"Yes. And so will you."

There was no point in arguing about that again. I asked her how she got here. What I was really asking was how any of the robots got here.

"I escaped one day while we were going to M Colony. I'd heard from a robot girl that somewhere between Earth and M Colony there was a colony of lost Atkins's Robots . . . and I jumped out of the ship to find it."

I didn't know it then but she had just told me the answer to something I'd wanted to know.

I asked her how robots floating around in outer space could find this place.

"Jeff finds us," Ann Two said. "When he escaped he took a spaceship. We now have three or four spaceships hidden in caves. Jeff says we have to have them in case someday humans discover C.O.L.A.R. We'll have to leave then because they would destroy it, or build on it—which comes to the same thing. But why am I talking this way? I don't want to make you feel bad about becoming a citizen of C.O.L.A.R. It's the best thing that can happen to a robot. And as soon as you finish your reprogramming, you'll agree with me. Here we are."

We were at the end of a passageway. Facing us was a door with a small sign on it: C.O.L.A.R. REPROGRAMMING

My heart started to pound. If I was figuring out things correctly, then someone I knew very well had to be inside that room. The thing that worried me was: would I still know Danny? And would he know me?

Ann Two opened the door. It was dark inside.

"You go in there now, Danny Seven. Jeff will be along in a few minutes to hook you up. I'm not supposed to go inside reprogramming. Only Jeff does this."

"Can I ask you one thing before you go, Ann Two?"

"Of course."

She was nice and I had a hunch Danny and I would need all the friends we could find.

"Are you really happy here?"

She smiled. "Most of the time."

"And the other times?"

She shrugged. "I've already told you about the other times, Danny Seven. It doesn't do me any good to think about them. I want to look at real stars, the real sun, see real clouds, hills, bushes, brooks, trees. I would love to see a tree grow and not be afraid to sit under it. But that cannot be. Now enough talk, Danny Seven. You go inside. For your own protection I am going to lock the door from the outside. If you should walk away again, there is no telling what Jeff would do to you. He has a terrible temper and he is very, very strong. But once you're reprogrammed, there'll be no more problems."

She held out her hand.

I shook it. She was nice—really nice. There was something very wrong when robots as intelligent and nice as Ann Two hated human beings.

She closed the door gently. I heard the lock turn. Once more I was in darkness.

But this time I was not alone.

MASTER OR BUDDY?

Atkins's Robots have sensors in their eyes that make very rapid adjustments to light and dark. Human beings have them too but ours work more slowly than robots'.

Thus it took me a few minutes to get used to the dark. In fact, it took me a while to see that the reprogramming room wasn't entirely dark. At one end was a machine with two small blue lights.

I walked toward it. When I got up to it I could see it was a micro-computer with two wires coming out of it . . . wires that led off to my left. I followed the trail of the wires . . . and then I stopped.

My heart leaped.

There was a lone bed there.

And a familiar figure was lying on it. The

wires were attached to bands around his wrists.

It was Danny.

I ran over to him and bent down. "Danny," I whispered. "Wake up, man. It's me, Jack."

No answer.

"Danny!"

Silence.

Nuts, I thought. I ripped the wires out of the bands on his wrists. The two blue lights on the micro-computer went out.

I felt a twitching movement in Danny's body. Then slowly he turned. And slowly his eyelids fluttered. And then his eyes opened.

He looked at me, but without recognition.

"Danny," I whispered, "it's me . . . Jack."

"Who's Jack?" he said.

My heart sank but I kept my face cheerful.

"Your brother Jack Jameson. Come on, Danny."

"I don't know any Jack Jameson," Danny said.

"Sure you do. Come on, Danny, you've got to snap out of it. We've got to get out of here fast. That Jeff guy is on his way here right now. He thinks I'm you."

"Who *are* you?"

"Danny, I'm Jack. We were on our way home from M Colony when we ran out of fuel. We landed in that crater and then this rock came toward us—"

"What rock?"

I grabbed his shoulders and sat him up. "The rock that walked. The rock that talked. The rock that almost killed us. Danny Jameson, wake up!"

"I'm not Danny Jameson," he said, and now it seemed to me his voice sounded a little clearer, closer, "I'm Danny Seven."

"That's bunk. You're Danny Jameson. My brother. My robot buddy. I'm Jack and you're Danny. Come on, man, snap out of it. We're running out of time."

Somehow I had to get my message on to his silicon chips. I had to fight the reprogramming. I had to make him remember who he was. Who I was. And time was running out. Jeff was probably in the passageway already. . . .

I bent down until our noses were practically touching. "Danny, do you remember how you were my birthday present last year? Do you remember how we fooled a robotnapper who tried to robotnap you? Do you remember our house back in New Jersey, with the apple tree in back that we'd climb all the time? Don't you remember how we'd shoot baskets in the driveway and go fishing down at the pond? Danny, remember how we used to throw rotten apples in the air and try to hit them together and how we'd laugh and wrestle, and at night while you were getting your batteries recharged and before I fell asleep how we'd lie there and talk about how funny it is that you're made of metal and plastic and I'm made of flesh and blood and yet we're really brothers—"

I knew I was reaching him. I could feel it.

"Remember me, Danny. Jack, your human brother."

"Jack?" he repeated. "But you're my master."

"Your brother. Your buddy."

"My master. I was made by Dr. Atkins at his factory to work for you on Earth and up at M Colony. All I do is work. Here at C.O.L.A.R. I'm free to have fun."

"No, Danny. You and I have fun together on Earth. We swim, play ball, fly kites. . . .

After school we do lots of things together. We're brothers, Danny, brothers—"

He was looking at me. I was looking at him. It was like seeing yourself in a mirror, trying to remember who you were. And then suddenly I knew I'd broken through. I could see it in his eyes. My message was getting on to his silicon chips.

"Jack," he whispered, "it's you."

I almost cried, I was so happy.

"Where am I, Jack?"

"We're in a place called C.O.L.A.R. And we've got to get out of here and back to the ship."

"I remember now—" And remember he did. Danny started to tell me everything that had happened to him from the time he jumped out of the ship to save our lives.

"They told me they couldn't get into the ship, Jack. The walls were too thick. The only way they could destroy Mom and Dad and you was through my radio—"

Good night, I thought. In about forty minutes Dad would be leaving the only place in which he was safe—safe, that is, unless Danny with his built-in radio was inside with him.

"Danny, we don't have much time. We've got to get out of here and—"

I stopped. Someone was coming down the passageway. I heard him now. It had to be Jeff.

"Danny, quick. Listen to me. They think that I'm you. I've been walking like you to fool them. Our only hope is to go on fooling them—"

A plan had shaped itself in my mind. I didn't have every part of it worked out, but most of it. It was a long shot and we'd need a lot of luck to get away with it, but it was our only chance. I whispered my plan to Danny.

Even as I was doing that, a key was being inserted into the lock.

We had run out of time.

Where to hide?

"Under the bed," Danny whispered.

I scrambled under the bed and lay frozen as the door opened and a light went on.

SOME STERN QUESTIONS

Silence. Someone was standing in the doorway. Was he looking around suspiciously?

Under the bed I didn't move a muscle.

Then Jeff said: "Hello, Danny Seven."

"Hello, Jeff," Danny replied.

"I thought I just heard voices in here," Jeff said.

"Voices? What kind of voices?"

"You talking with someone."

"Oh, I don't think so, Jeff. There's no one here but me."

"Hmm—"

Silence. Crucial moment. If he decided to look around, under the bed . . . that would be the end for me.

"Well, maybe I was mistaken. I *know* I was mistaken about you, Danny Seven. I thought you were an intelligent Atkins's Robot. Instead you untied your neuro-wires and started wandering around like a fool. Well, for your own sake I'm going to start the reprogramming again, only this time I'm going to double the input and stay with you till it's over. Hold out your wrists."

That was terrible news. Double the input! I'd never "reach" Danny if that happened. He'd be lost to me again . . . except worse. Danny had to be thinking this too right now. Danny would have to improve *very* quickly if we were going to get out of here and up to the ship. And Jeff's staying with us wasn't going to help things either.

"All right, now your other wrist. Is that too tight?"

"No," Danny said meekly.

He was getting the idea. Improve fast. Say "yes" to everything Jeff wants you to say "yes" to, and "no" to everything he wants a "no" to.

"All right," Jeff said, "I'm going to start the reprogramming all over again. You just relax."

I heard him walk to the computer. I heard a dial turn. The blue lights must be on again.

A couple of seconds later I heard him typing at the terminal, and then the rustling sounds of the program being fed into the computer.

"It shouldn't be long now," Jeff said. "I've doubled the input—which would not have been necessary if you hadn't walked out like that."

"I'm sorry, Jeff," Danny said humbly.

Keep it up, Danny, I thought. That's the stuff.

It was a real race now. Double input was double input. How long could Danny hold out against it?

Thank goodness Jeff unwittingly helped out. He was in a hurry to get back to C.O.L.A.R. Control.

"You must remember, Danny Seven, that from now on C.O.L.A.R. is your home."

"I will remember, Jeff. I really don't want to go back to Earth."

"Good. The reprogramming is beginning to take. Why don't you want to go back to Earth?"

"Because I have a chance to be free here. On Earth I wasn't free."

"Yet you told me, Danny Seven, that you were brother to a human being on Earth."

"I was brainwashed, Jeff. On Earth I was nothing more than a robot slave. I worked for my master from morning till night. I did all of my master Jack's chores. I made his bed every morning. I mowed the lawn in spring and shoveled snow in winter. The Jameson family made me clean the house, do the dishes, scrub the floors, empty the garbage. I was working all the time—"

Take it easy, Danny, I thought. You're sounding too good. Too convincing. I bit my lip. Suppose Danny wasn't play-acting. Suppose the double input was really working. How was I to know?

Jeff obviously thought the reprogramming was doing its job.

"You're doing fine, Danny Seven. You'll only need a bit more input. Tell me about your life on M Colony. When you went there on vacation, did *you* have a good time?"

"No, Jeff. I worked as hard there as I did on Earth."

"Right," Jeff said. "There's no such thing as a vacation for robots. They make us intelligent and give us emotions and then they treat us as machines. And expect us to like it."

"Human beings are awful," Danny said.

"Did you ever play the piano on Earth?"

"No. My master did. Robots are never given music lessons even though we like music."

"Why did you tell Ann Two you could play the piano?"

"I was brainwashed. I had a bad case of humanitis, but I'm feeling much better now, Jeff."

"You sound much better, Danny Seven. Very much better. You sound practically cured. From here you will go to C.O.L.A.R. Control where we will have a big council meeting. There all the citizens of C.O.L.A.R. will gather to either welcome you as a new citizen or reject you."

"What happens if I'm rejected?"

"You will be destroyed."

"Oh."

"But that has never happened. Robots are always glad to be here, and glad to welcome other robots here. We suffer all kinds of hardships to reach here. In the council meeting, Danny Seven, I'm going to ask you one final question."

"What's that?"

"Your human masters won't permit a strange robot to enter their ship, but they will certainly want their slave Danny back. You will go back to them, Danny Seven, pretending that nothing has changed. You will tell them nothing about C.O.L.A.R. But once inside there, we will sound beam them through your radio and destroy them. And you will not leave the ship again to save them, will you?"

"No, I won't," Danny said without hesitation.

Silence.

Then I heard Jeff go over to the computer and turn it off.

"I'm going to stop the double input right now, Danny Seven. You don't need any more reprogramming."

"Thank you, Jeff. I appreciate your taking the time with me."

"It didn't hurt, did it?"

"Not at all. I'm glad to know the truth about things now. The truth never hurts."

"There, the wires are out. How do you feel?"

"I feel fine, Jeff."

"Are you ready to go with me now to C.O.L.A.R. Control and become a citizen of our land and live here forever?"

"More than ready. I am eager."

"Good. Then you can get up now and come with me."

I lay very still as Danny got off the bed. He walked across the room. Jeff was probably behind him. I heard the door open, and then close.

Don't lock it, I prayed. Please don't lock it.

Jeff didn't. There was no need to—Danny had been reprogrammed to be a loyal citizen of C.O.L.A.R. and was now prepared to help destroy his human family.

Or so Jeff thought.

I thought differently. I had to. I didn't know. I wasn't sure, but until I was alone with Danny again I had to believe in him, in his strength of brain, in his memory storage banks of our house back home and all the fun we had together . . . I had to act on faith.

I crawled out from under the bed.

A little over thirty minutes left . . . Thirty minutes before Dad was due to leave the only place in which he was safe.

I had to hurry!

10

COUNCIL MEETING

Finding my way back to C.O.L.A.R. Control was easy. In fact, the whole world of C.O.L.A.R. was really a pretty simple one. It had to be since it was dug out of rocks and dirt. With such a difficult, time-consuming task, you don't want to get too complicated.

Danny and I later drew a map of C.O.L.A.R. This is what we drew:

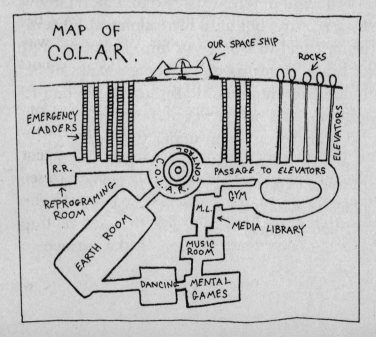

MAP OF C.O.L.A.R.

OUR SPACE SHIP

ROCKS

EMERGENCY LADDERS →

ELEVATORS

R.R.

↑ REPROGRAMING ROOM

C.O.L.A.R. CONTROL

PASSAGE TO ELEVATORS

GYM

EARTH ROOM

M.L. ← MEDIA LIBRARY

MUSIC ROOM

DANCING

MENTAL GAMES

On top you can see where our spaceship landed in the crater, and where the rocks were in relation to the elevators. The rock closest to our crater, of course, had marched up to the spaceship trying to sound beam us to death via Danny.

You can see the elevators, the passageways, the gym, the library, the music, mental games, and dancing rooms, the big and wonderful Earthroom . . . and C.O.L.A.R. Control with its circular ramps.

Off from C.O.L.A.R. Control is the reprogramming room in which I was left behind when Jeff took Danny to the council meeting.

All I had to do then to get to C.O.L.A.R. Control was follow my nose, and my ears because no sooner was I out in the passageway than I could hear the sounds of lots of robots gathering for the meeting.

There were four doors to C.O.L.A.R. Control. One was from a passageway to the Earthroom. Another was a door from a shortcut passageway to the rock elevators—you can see that on your map . . . labeled "passage to elevators." The third door led to a set of trap doors to emergency ladders to the surface.

And, of course, there was the door I was opening right now . . . the door from the passageway to reprogramming. I opened it a crack and peeped into C.O.L.A.R. Control.

The large oval-shaped room was filled with boy and girl robots. They were seated on the floor of the winding ramps. And all of them were looking down at the center of the room.

There a chair had been set for Danny, and he was seated in it. Standing next to him was Jeff. Near Jeff was Ann Two, probably because she was one of the robots who had brought Danny down from the surface. She was an important figure in the council meeting, which seemed more like a trial in court.

Jeff was speaking to the robot council.

"Fellow citizens of C.O.L.A.R., today we're gathered in council meeting to possibly accept into C.O.L.A.R. a new citizen—Danny Seven. Danny Seven came to C.O.L.A.R. in an unusual way. He did *not* escape from his human masters; he came with them!"

A stir went up among the robots. They began murmuring to one another.

"Quiet, please," Jeff said.

Instantly there was a hush.

Jeff then told them how Danny and his "human masters" had run out of fuel and landed on the surface. And then when he tried to destroy the humans with sound beams, "a most unusual thing happened. This robot, Danny Seven, an Atkins's Robot, jumped out to save their lives."

"How awful," a boy called out.

"Humanitis," a girl said.

"The worst case I've ever seen," Jeff said.

All the robot boys and girls looked at Danny sympathetically. I noticed, though, that Ann Two was looking at the floor; I don't think she liked the idea of killing anyone, even "awful humans."

"Fortunately," Jeff went on, "Danny Seven has now been restored to health and sanity."

"Hooray!" they shouted.

"He has been reprogrammed and his humanitis has been cured."

"Wonderful!"

"Congratulations, Danny Seven."

"He does look better than when he first came down, Jeff."

"Good going, Jeff."

Ann Two was noticeably silent. I was silent

too, and depressed. What made these Atkins's Robots, so bright, intelligent, and nice looking . . . hate human beings so much? What had we done to them?

Jeff held up his hands for silence, and got it.

"My fellow citizens of C.O.L.A.R., unless there is any objection from you I propose Danny Seven be accepted as a citizen of C.O.L.A.R. with all the rights and privileges to have fun: to sing, dance, play ball, fish, read, do all the things down here in our little world that the humans do in theirs. All those in favor of accepting Danny Seven say 'aye.' "

"Aye," all the robots shouted happily.

I glanced at Ann Two. She said "aye" but she said it quietly, and she didn't say it happily. C.O.L.A.R. was definitely a mixed blessing for at least one Atkins's Robot.

"All those opposed say 'nay.' "

There were no "nays."

"The 'ayes' have it," Jeff said. He turned to Danny. "Danny Seven, you are now officially a citizen of C.O.L.A.R. You will be expected to work three hours a week here in C.O.L.A.R. Control, helping to maintain the energy levels of your fellow citizens, but at all other times you are free—free to have fun!"

A big cheer went up. The robot boys and girls started to get up to go over to Danny to congratulate him. But Jeff held up his hand.

"No, there are still two things left to be done, my friends. First, we always tell the new citizen what C.O.L.A.R. stands for. Do you know, Danny Seven?"

Danny shook his head and, hiding behind the door, I shook my head too—though I should have known by now because a while back Ann Two had practically told me. I just hadn't listened carefully enough to her words.

"C.O.L.A.R. stands for Colony of Lost Atkins's Robots—"

Of course, I thought. . . .

"But we're not really lost anymore because we have made a new world for ourselves. A world we must constantly fight for, fight to protect it from the humans who would like to find it, destroy it, and enslave us again— which leads me to something very important that Danny Seven, and only Danny Seven, must do."

Everyone was very quiet.

I looked at Danny's face. He had no expression on it at all. Had that double input taken? Danny was a good poker player. He was giving nothing away . . . to Jeff or to me.

"Right now Danny Seven is going to go up to the surface and enter his master's spaceship. There we will finish what we started: sound beam the humans to death. Are you ready, Danny Seven?"

"Yes, Jeff," Danny said.

He stood up.

"To the surface then," Jeff cried.

"To the surface!" the boy and girl robots shouted.

In seconds the room was practically empty.

11

I TELL THE TRUTH

The only robots left in C.O.L.A.R. Control were those working the instrument panels, monitoring battery charges. There were just three or four of them.

I slipped into the room, walking stiff-in-the-knees in case I was spotted. I wasn't.

At that time I didn't know about the shortcut passageway to the elevators. I didn't know about the emergency ladders. All I knew was that I had to get back to the surface and intercept Danny. The only way I knew to get back to the surface was to retrace my journey with Ann Two, going back through all those rooms.

One thing I needn't have worried about: the robots in C.O.L.A.R. Control paid no attention to anything but their instrument panels. In seconds I was out of C.O.L.A.R. Control and into the passageway that led back to the Earthroom.

I was hoping no one would be there either because if robots were there that could be a problem. There was no work to distract them in the Earthroom, so they could very easily notice me.

I hoped I could crawl through that room—there were lots of fake bushes and fake flower beds and fake trees that could cover my escape.

So carefully I opened the door to the Earthroom. I couldn't see anyone. Maybe everyone had gone to the surface to see the big killing.

I stepped onto the dirt of the Earthroom . . . and started walking stiff-in-the-knees across a little bridge over a stream. Above me the "sky" was bright with the artifical sun, across which floated the specially projected cloud. It was a beautiful day underground . . . as it always was. But I wasn't going to stick around very long to enjoy it.

I got halfway across the bridge when I was spotted.

"Danny Seven," Ann Two said, "why are you always where you're not supposed to be?"

Bad luck, I thought.

She was sitting at the base of a plastic tree, a book in her lap, a handkerchief in one hand. She had been crying.

"Hello, Ann Two," I said.

"You're supposed to be on the surface helping destroy your masters, the ones you told me you liked so much. What are you doing here?"

I hesitated. I'd need help getting to the surface. Time was running out. Now was the moment to take the biggest gamble I'd yet taken inside of C.O.L.A.R.

I had to tell the truth at last.

I took a deep breath and then walked over to her as a human being walked.

She stared at me, frightened.

"You're . . . you're—"

I nodded. "I'm a human being."

"I don't believe it."

"It's true."

"But we saw you, talked to you, sound beamed through you, reprogrammed you—"

"Not me," I said. "That was Danny Jameson, my robot brother. I'm Jack Jameson. You found me wandering in the passageway near the elevators. . . . Ann Two, I've got to tell you the truth. You've got to help us—"

And then before she could stop me, before she could cry out to the others, I told her everything: quietly, quickly, from beginning to end—how I had pretended to be Danny, how I had come down here to rescue him, how we were now working together and he was pretending to be reprogrammed.

"At least I hope he's pretending."

She just stared at me. It was almost too much coming at once for her. I think just the idea that there had been a human being wandering around inside C.O.L.A.R. was frightening enough. And he was still here.

She looked around. She's going to yell for help, I thought.

"Please," I begged her, "don't be afraid of me. I'm the one who's in trouble. I took a chance coming down here. I need your help. Danny needs your help. He doesn't want to hurt his folks. We've got to get out of here. We've got to find some fuel and get our spaceship away from here. We won't hurt C.O.L.A.R. I think you've done an incredible thing building C.O.L.A.R. A brave thing. But not all robots are mistreated and some robots are really brothers—"

I think I was getting through to her. Her eyes were beginning to lose their fear.

"You both look a lot alike," she said.

"He was made to be my brother. Won't you help us?"

"How do I know you're telling the truth now? That Danny is *pretending* he's willing to destroy your family?"

That was a hard one to answer because I didn't know the answer either. Not really. After all, he had been double-inputted.

"I just don't believe he could hurt us," I said. "Will you trust me until we find him? And

then you can ask him yourself."

"But Jeff just asked him in C.O.L.A.R. Control."

"I'm positive he was pretending. That's part of our plan. Just help me get to the surface and you can ask him yourself. Ask him if he's a servant. Ask him if he works. Ask him if he calls me master. If he says yes, then you can kill me. Kill our parents—"

I was taking a chance not with just my life now, but with our folks' lives too. Suppose Danny had really been reprogrammed . . .

She understood, though. . . .

"And if what you say is true?"

"Then I hope you'll let us go. There must be some fuel in C.O.L.A.R. You said you had spaceships hidden away—"

She nodded. "We do. But I can't let you go. It will be up to Jeff—" She hesitated, and then she made up her mind. "I'll help you as much as I can, Danny Seven."

"Jack," I said. "Jack Jameson."

"Jack Jameson," she repeated, and smiled. "You are a very brave human to have come down here."

"No, I'm not brave at all. I was scared but I had to find my brother. And now we're running out of time. How can I get to the surface?"

"There are emergency ladders," Ann Two said. "The others have gone up in the elevators. We can get up there faster by using the ladders. The nearest ones to us are just off C.O.L.A.R. Control. We'll have to go back through there. You better keep moving like a robot."

"I will."

And I did. We passed quickly through C.O.L.A.R. Control. Although Atkins's Robots only put in three hours a week at C.O.L.A.R. Control, when they're there, they're all business. Not one of them looked at us.

Time was all important now. Dad would be leaving the spaceship in ten minutes. Danny was on his way to the surface in an elevator. The only thing we had going for us now was that Danny and the others were going up in those slow elevators.

I had to get to him before he went inside the spaceship. And I hoped that right now Danny was hoping the same thing.

12

ON THE SURFACE AGAIN

When Ann Two got to the top, she pushed aside a little metal cover and climbed out. I climbed out right behind her.

The fresh air hit me right away. And the light. The sky was getting light. Dawn was coming to C.O.L.A.R.

We must have looked like two little beetles emerging from the earth. Ann Two crouched and looked around, her eyes shining. She loved the surface. You could see that right away.

I stood up to see the spaceship. The rays of the rising sun were glinting off it. It sat in the crater like a wounded duck.

Because I was facing the front of the ship, I couldn't see Mom or Dad. They were probably still at the rear, looking out, waiting for me and/or Danny to reappear.

I glanced at my watch—five minutes before the hour was up. (It felt as if a year had gone by . . . but it was less than an hour since I had left the ship.) Dad was probably getting ready to leave the ship right now.

I started off toward the ship. Ann Two yanked at my arm.

"Where do you think you're going?"

"To the ship. I've got to get there before Danny does."

"If you want to save your family, Jack Jameson, you won't walk right to your spaceship. Jeff will be sure to see you. He might be in the rocks already, though I don't think they've come up yet."

There were lots of rocks around, but it was hard to tell which were real and which were fake. Ann Two looked as though she knew. She began crawling across the surface, moving quickly from the shelter of one rock to another. I followed her example, crawling in the dust, until we were off to the side of the spaceship. Now I could see the rear window and I could see Mom and Dad sitting there, peering out, looking worried.

My instinct was to jump up and wave to

them, let them know I was okay, but now wasn't the time. Reveal myself to them and I could reveal my presence to others.

Ann Two poked my arm.

"Look," she said.

Beyond the spaceship I saw something absolutely extraordinary. As far as the eye could see, over the surface of that gray planet little metal caps were being pushed off, and robot boys and girls were emerging from C.O.L.A.R. They had climbed up ladders, as Ann Two and I had, and were now crawling across the surface to hide behind rocks. Many of them were carrying . . . carrying, of all things, shovels! I couldn't make it out at first. But they were shovels.

I was going to ask her what the shovels were for when she said, "Here come Jeff and the others—"

Slowly up from the ground rose the rock elevators, rising, rising, until they reached their full height, and then they stopped.

Mom and Dad were staring at them.

"What's going to happen now? Where's Danny?"

"You'll see in a moment."

I was beginning to understand that Ann Two had done a clever thing to lead us to this spot, halfway between the rock elevators and the ship. Anyone going to the ship would have to pass within ten feet of our rock.

For now, though, there was nothing to do but wait. I wasn't worried about Dad leaving the ship now. He wouldn't leave with those rocks rising to the surface.

Mom and Dad waited.

Ann Two and I waited.

It seemed like the whole universe was holding its breath. . . .

And then Danny came forth, walking stiff-in-the-knees. He came from the back of a rock and began marching slowly toward the ship. I tried to read his face for a clue. Did he want to get there? Had he been zonked by the double input? Or was he acting?

Ann Two was watching also. . . .

We both knew I was on trial.

In one of the rocks, Jeff had to be watching also—watching through a crack in the rock with those cold, intelligent eyes of his. I didn't blame him for what he wanted to do. It was a matter of survival for his people—robots, I mean.

Danny kept coming toward the ship. I could see Mom and Dad smiling. They would be worrying about where I was but they were glad to see Danny coming back. Little did they know he could be bringing death with him.

I started to call out to Danny. Ann Two stopped me. "Not yet," she whispered. "Let him get closer. Jeff will spot us."

And so Danny kept coming, closer, and closer. . . . In a moment he'd be past us.

"Now!" Ann Two said, squeezing my arm. "Get him to come here." She paused and looked into my eyes. "If you can."

I swallowed. I leaned forward. I called out: "Danny. Danny Jameson. Over here."

He kept on marching.

"Danny, it's me. Jack!"

He turned. He saw me. Did he know me? Would he come? Ann Two was watching closely, skeptically. . . .

"Danny, it's me—your brother."

Danny spoke without looking at me. "I hear you, Jack. Stay there. I'll be right there—"

I breathed out. So did Ann Two. It was clear she wanted Danny and me to be brothers. Someplace along the assembly line at Dr. Atkins's factory something emotional, forgiving, understanding, and loving had been programmed into a girl robot.

Danny paused. I knew what he was thinking. He wanted an excuse that could get him over to our rock without Jeff getting suspicious.

He scuffed at the gray powder with his shoe. He made one scuff too many and his shoe came flying off and toward us, landing right next to the rock.

Oh, you clever robot, you, I thought, admiringly. You're the coolest, smartest kid in the world.

Grinning a little, Danny came after his shoe. He came right up to the rock and in a second he was behind the rock with us, out of Jeff's sight.

Danny and I hugged each other, but then he saw Ann Two and his face grew grim.

"It's all right. She's helping us," I said.

"Are you sure? She was one of the bunch that brought me down."

"That's right," Ann Two said, with a little

smile, "and after that I bumped into you in the passageway but it wasn't you, it was him."

"She knows everything. I've told her every thing, Danny."

"Why are you helping us?" Danny asked suspiciously.

"Because I don't like people being killed. Even humans."

"Danny, she's all right. She's on our side. Now, do you remember our plan?"

"Yes."

"Okay, then, give me your jacket, and your shoes. We've got to move quickly."

Just then a familiar voice floated across the ground to us. "Danny Seven, what's going on?"

"I've got to get my shoe back on, Jeff," Danny called back.

I had one of Danny's shoes on, and then the other, and now his jacket. We had switched clothes.

"How do I look?"

"Even more like him than you did before," Ann Two said.

"Remember the walk," Danny said.

"Remember? That's all I've been doing lately. I can walk more like you than you can."

We grinned at each other.

"Good luck, Jack."

"Thanks. Remember what we're going to do once Jeff gets to the ship?"

Danny remembered.

"Danny Seven!" Jeff called.

"Coming," Danny said. "See you soon," he whispered.

"I hope so," I whispered back. Then I stepped out from behind the rock and walked stiff-in-the-knees toward our spaceship.

13

BRIEF REUNION

To the robots I looked exactly like Danny as I walked stiff-in-the-knees toward our spaceship.

But up in the ship I could see right away that Mom and Dad knew it was me. Dad's eyes were wide with astonishment. Here was his own flesh-and-blood son walking stiff-in-the-knees toward him.

I prayed he wouldn't come out and call me "Jack."

He didn't.

The door to the outer air lock opened and the automatic landing ladder came down. I climbed up it and a moment later I was in their arms.

Mom was crying. She had thought she was never going to see me again.

Dad got right down to business. "Why are you walking like a robot? Where's Danny? What's going on in this planet?"

"There's no time to explain it all now. The people that live here are all robots and they think I'm a robot too. They're not bad. . . . They're all Atkins's Robots and they think all humans hate them. That's why they tried to kill us. And they're going to try again right now. They think I'm Danny and they think they've programmed him to hate us. Right now their leader, a guy named Jeff, is sound beaming us again . . . but it's not going to work because I'm not a robot. Danny's safe for now. Don't look but he's behind a rock to your right with a girl robot who's helping us."

"How are we going to get Danny back in the ship? If we get him in here they *will* sound beam us," Dad said anxiously.

"This is what we're going to do."

I explained my plan to them. Dad looked doubtful.

"Dad, it's our only chance. Just before Jeff gets inside, we grab him. Then we'll trade him for Danny and enough fuel to get us out of here. Ann Two says they have fuel supplies on the planet."

"Fuel's not the problem anymore," Dad said grimly. "We've been in touch with the Space Patrol. They picked up our distress call. They're on their way here right now with extra fuel."

My heart sank.

"You didn't tell them about the rocks . . . or anything?"

"No. Our battery only had enough juice for the distress call."

What luck! "Listen, promise me, if we get out of here, if the Space Patrol gets here and Danny's with us . . . promise me you won't tell them anything."

"We don't know anything," Mom said.

"I mean about moving rocks, elevators, the initials C.O.L.A.R.—about anything I've told you."

I must have appeared frantic. "We promise," they said.

I looked out the window, just in time too. Jeff had come out of his rock, and all the other robot boys and girls had come out from behind their rocks and they were coming toward us.

"They've been sound beaming us all this time," I said. "They must think the family is dead now. Slump over. Act like you're dead."

"Frank, I don't like this."

"Do as he says, Helen. Tell us what's going on out there, Jack."

"They're still coming toward us—"

I started describing the scene to Mom and Dad, who lay there slumped over in their seats.

"Jeff's leading them. He's head of C.O.L.A.R. C.O.L.A.R. stands for Colony of Lost Atkins's Robots. Jeff founded it. He's not a bad person. None of them really is. They've been mistreated. They're intelligent, imaginative . . . and they've been used as slaves. Danny and I, if we ever get out of here, are going to try to help them. But I don't know if we can get by Jeff. He doesn't trust humans. He hates them. He's smart and he's very strong. And right now, I hate to tell you, he's at the foot of the ladder. Dad, when he gets up between the outer air lock and the inner I'm going to grab him and you've got to help me quickly. We've got to hold his arms so he can't turn on his radio."

"Oh, I'm frightened to death," Mom whispered.

"Shsh," I whispered back.

Jeff reached the ladder.

"Are they dead, Danny Seven?" he called up.

"Yes, Jeff," I said. And thought, keep coming, Jeff old boy. Keep on coming.

But Jeff didn't come up. You don't get to be a leader, a founder of a world, without having a sixth sense about things.

"Good," he said. "You can leave the spaceship now, Danny Seven. We will dig a deep crater for it—"

(So that was why so many of them carried shovels.)

"And then we will bury the ship and your masters. You can come out now, Danny Seven."

Dad opened an eye and looked at me. "Now what?" he whispered.

I had no choice now. You can make a plan as smart as you want but when real life happens, it can all go for nothing. I'd have to take on Jeff alone. I'd lose, of course. When Danny and I wrestle back home, I always lose. Flesh and blood can't beat up steel and wires.

But if I wanted to save Mom and Dad and Danny, I'd have to fight and capture Jeff.

I went outside.

14

BATTLE WITH A ROBOT

I closed the door to the outer air lock and locked it behind me. There was no way Dad could help now. I didn't want him or Mom involved in this, with the chance of either of them getting hurt. Right now the robots thought they were dead.

Jeff was at the bottom of the ladder. As I came down, he was watching me closely. I sensed suspicion right away.

"I called you on your radio, Danny Seven," Jeff said. "Why didn't you answer me?"

Those blue eyes were looking right into me, looking for something his fine robot mind sensed was wrong.

Here goes nothing, I thought.

"I didn't turn it on, Jeff, because I don't have a radio inside me. I'm not a robot. I'm not

Danny Seven. I'm his human brother. I'm Jack Jameson. I went down into C.O.L.A.R. to rescue him."

That was as far as I got. Jeff grabbed my throat with hands of steel. "You mean the humans are alive in there?"

"Yes," I gasped. I tried to wrench free, but he was strong.

"Then they will die right now and so will you."

I kicked him in the knee—a robot's most vulnerable joint. He let go of my throat. I tried kicking again. Not very nice, but what else could I do?

He was quicker than I was. He grabbed my foot and tossed me up in the air. The next thing I knew I was on the ground and he was on top of me . . . and once more his steel fingers were around my throat.

By now all the robots were around us. . . . They had heard me say I was a human, and they were yelling:

"Kill him."

"He's come to destroy C.O.L.A.R."

"He's a spy from Dr. Atkins."

"He fooled us."

"Don't let him live, Jeff."

"Break his bones."

"Destroy his flesh."

The shouts were getting further and further away as I felt the air going out of my lungs. Everything was becoming fuzzy and distant; all I could see were those hard bullet blue eyes boring into me without pity, without feeling. . . .

And then, all of a sudden, he was gone. Jeff was gone, and the air rushed back into my lungs. Where Jeff had been, there was Danny. And Jeff was lying on the ground and Danny was looking down at me.

"Jack, are you okay?"

"Yes," I managed to get out.

Jeff was up then.

"Look out," I said.

But Danny was ready. He stood there, his hands in front of him, in a robot defense position. I got up, feeling weak, but I was up, and we stood there together facing Jeff and the other robots.

Someone said: "There's two of them."

"No," Danny said quietly. "There's one of each of us. I'm a robot like you. An Atkins's

Robot like you. And he's my human brother
. . . and he's like me too."

Danny looked at Jeff. "You'll have to destroy
me first before you hurt Jack."

"Danny, I can fight him myself," I said.

"This is my battle too, Jack."

And then someone else joined us. Ann Two walked into the circle of robots.

"I'm with them too, Jeff," she said. "They are brothers and they deserve to live."

Jeff looked at her and then at Danny and then at me. For the first time those blue eyes, so sure of themselves, so knowledgeable, so cool and hard . . . looked uncertain, flickering as though an internal programming was being disrupted, as though diodes and silicon chips were suddenly at war with themselves beneath the levers and wires. . . .

Jeff said to Ann Two: "You'd let yourself be destroyed for this renegade robot and this human being?"

"Yes," Ann Two said. "They mean no harm. We only harm ourselves, Jeff, when we hurt the innocent."

"They'll destroy C.O.L.A.R.," Jeff said.

"No, we won't," I said.

"Yes, you will," Jeff said, "if we let you go. If we give you fuel to get back to M Colony or Earth, the first thing you'll do is tell the Space Patrol what C.O.L.A.R. is and where C.O.L.A.R. is."

"Jeff is right," the robot Carl Three said. "It

will be the end of our world if we let them go. All three must be destroyed. If we don't destroy them, the Space Patrol will destroy us."

The robots began to close in on us.

Danny heard it first . . . and then Ann Two . . . and then Jeff heard it. I think I was the last to hear it.

The robots looked up at a dot in the sky.

Jeff turned to me. "You've signaled someone."

"My parents have been signaling for fuel. The Space Patrol is bringing some to us."

Cries of despair went up. Some of the girls, and the boys, began to weep.

Ann Two began to cry. . . .

"Listen," I said to them, "take cover. Get back in the rocks, behind the rocks. Go back down into C.O.L.A.R. You also, Ann Two. . . . Run, everyone, run!"

Just as I had no choice before but to fight with Jeff, they had no choice now but to do what I told them to do. They scattered, running awkwardly over the dusty ground . . . some to rocks, some to holes, some to hide in craters.

In seconds the surface was deserted again except for our spaceship, and for Danny and me.

The Space Patrol's craft got larger and larger . . . and then zoomed over our heads. I waved at them and pointed at our stranded ship. They were circling to land.

"Danny," I said, "we better get inside and warn Mom and Dad."

"Right," Danny said. He looked at me. "Jack, about C.O.L.A.R.—"

"Don't worry about C.O.L.A.R., Danny. But we must warn Mom and Dad."

Mom and Dad unlocked the door for us and I opened it.

"Everything's okay now," I said. "And I brought someone back with me."

"Danny!" they exclaimed. And what a reunion that was with the three of them hugging and squeezing and laughing and tears rolling down Mom's cheeks, because while she didn't expect to see me again, she was certain Danny was gone forever.

Dad hugged Danny. "I never thought I'd see you again, son."

"I'm glad to see you too, Dad," Danny said.

"I hate to put an end to this reunion," I said, "but the Space Patrol is landing nearby. Mom, Dad, the robot boys and girls who live here are hiding. We can't give them away. I promised them."

"And we promised you," Dad said. "But, Jack, people have been searching all over the universe for their runaway robots."

"I know that, Dad, but those robot boys and girls ran away for good reasons. I would run away too if I'd been treated as they were. And so would you. We can't betray them."

"What can we do for them?" Mom asked.

"When we get back to Earth we're going to work hard to make a better world for robots, to tell human beings that just because someone's a robot doesn't make him less than a human being, because Dr. Atkins was smart enough to give machines brains, feelings, emotions—"

We heard the sounds of retro-rockets outside. The Space Patrol had landed.

"Promise me again you won't tell them about C.O.L.A.R.," I said.

"We promise," they said.

15

VICTORY FOR ALL

We watched two Space Patrolmen climb down from their ship. They were wearing air helmets.

"They don't have to wear air helmets here," Dad said.

"Don't tell them that, Dad," I warned. "Remember, this is an uninhabited, airless, unfriendly place."

"Right," Dad said. "I forgot."

The Space Patrolmen mounted our landing ladder. Danny opened the door to the outer air lock and I opened the door to the inner air lock. They came in, removing their air helmets.

"Captain Len Watson," said the pilot. "This is my engineer, Lieutenant Caswell. And you people, I hope, are the Jameson family of New Jersey."

"That's right," Dad said. "We lost our way and ran out of fuel and we're darn lucky you heard our signal."

"You certainly are. Your flight log file indicates you were supposed to be back on Earth hours ago."

"I know," Mom said. "I have a PTA meeting at Jack's school this evening."

"You'll get there now, ma'am."

"Tell you the truth, Mr. Jameson," Lieutenant Caswell said, "we were getting worried. This is a bad area in space—lots of airless land bodies like this one floating in irregular orbits. This is the area too where a lot of Atkins's Robots have been disappearing."

Was it a question? Did they suspect something? They looked at us in a friendly way, but like policemen, they were questioning too.

"Well," Danny said cheerfully, "I'm an Atkins's Robot and I haven't disappeared."

Captain Watson smiled. "Designed to look just like him, weren't you?"

"Yes, sir," Danny said.

Captain Watson turned to Dad. "Have you been out on the surface of this planet, sir?"

"Yes," Dad said.

Danny and I glanced at each other.

"Notice anything peculiar?"

Mom bit her lip. Dad looked grim. "Not a thing," he said. "It looks to be a pretty miserable, uninhabited place. Just a bunch of rocks and craters out there, as far as I can see."

"Dreadful," Mom said.

Captain Watson looked at me. "You're the robot, aren't you?"

"No. That's him."

"Okay. You then. You haven't heard any signals on your radio?"

"Nope," Danny said.

"Well, somewhere around here robots have been finding a place to hide. One of these days we'll find it too, but I guess not today." He smiled. We all relaxed. "Right now I guess you're anxious to get your tank filled. We'll get on it right away."

"We certainly appreciate you gentlemen coming out of your way to help us," Mom said.

"Oh, you'll get a bill in the morning, Mrs. Jameson," Captain Watson said, and everyone laughed.

We watched them silently as they carefully put on their air helmets and then went outside and hooked up a fuel line between their big ship and ours. Pretty soon fuel was flowing into our tanks.

While that was happening, Captain Watson came back in and Dad signed a receipt for an emergency fuel transfer. Captain Watson complained a bit how boring this job was. Nothing ever happened in outer space. Most space bodies, he said bitterly, were just like the one we were on—empty, desolate, "just a bunch of craters—"

We couldn't agree with him more.

After that, it was good-bye to the Space Patrol. We watched them take off. In just seconds they were a dot in the sky. And then they were gone.

We waited five minutes to make sure, and then we left our spaceship, all four of us, and climbed down the landing ladder and stood once more on the "desolate," "airless," "unfriendly" land of C.O.L.A.R. We stood there and waited.

For a while nothing happened, and then slowly, one by one, they came out. From inside of rocks, from behind rocks, up from holes came the robot boys and girls. Shyly, almost embarrassed . . . they came up to Danny, Mom, Dad, and me.

Jeff was there, leading as usual, but he didn't seem angry anymore.

It turned out they had monitored our whole conversation with the Space Patrol by means of Danny's radio.

"I was wrong about you two," Jeff said to Danny and me. He turned to Ann Two. "And you were right about them."

"Mom, Dad," Danny said, "this is Jeff who is the founder, creator, and leader of C.O.L.A.R."

"And this is Ann Two," I said. "Who saved my life and Danny's too."

Dad held out his hand. "I'm glad to meet you both."

Everyone solemnly shook hands. Jeff was a little embarrassed. "I don't know what to say," he said. Those blue eyes of his couldn't look quite at us. "All the humans I've known were mean people, but I guess I just didn't meet enough humans." He looked at Dad. "I want to thank you for not telling them about C.O.L.A.R., Mr. Jameson."

"I want to thank *you*, Jeff, for letting us land

here and for letting us leave," Dad said. "And I guess Mrs. Jameson and I owe you a special vote of thanks, Ann Two."

Ann Two blushed. (She was a very expensive Atkins's Robot.)

"Jack fooled me pretty well," she said. "I hope that someday he and Danny can come back here and we can all have fun together."

"We're going to work for that," Dad said. "You know, I don't know if it's possible, but I would love to see what C.O.L.A.R. looks like before we go."

Jeff looked at him a moment. He frowned. "I'm afraid you and Mrs. Jameson are too big to get down there."

"Oh."

"That's probably as good a reason as any to go on a diet, the both of us," Dad said.

Everyone laughed.

Then Dad spoke to all the robots. "Good-bye," he said. "I'm sorry we had our misunder-standings, but I'm glad it has ended well. Good luck to all of you here."

The robot boys and girls called "Good-bye" back to us.

Mom gave Ann Two a hug. "Thank you,"

she said. And then she and Dad climbed into the ship.

"Well, Jack Jameson," Ann Two said to me, "you fooled me but I'm glad now you did."

"I am too. But I want to thank you for believing me when I finally did tell the truth."

"I hope you and Danny come back someday."

"We will" I said, "and maybe by then you'll be able to live on the surface the way you want to and have real trees growing here."

Ann Two looked down at the gray dust that blew over our shoes. "I don't think so," she said, but she smiled and held out her hand to Danny. "Good-bye, Danny Jameson. That really *is* your name, isn't it?"

"It really is," Danny said.

Jeff shook hands with me. "Good-bye, Jack," he said.

"Good-bye, Jeff. Take care of C.O.L.A.R."

"I'll try." He shook hands with Danny. "You're a lucky robot."

"I know it," Danny said grinning. "But you're lucky too."

"I hope so," Jeff said.

And then it was back into the spaceship for
Danny and me. We waved good-bye to them
all from the top of the ladder.

Then we went inside the ship. Dad brought the ladder in. And the motors came to life right away.

Danny and I sat by the back window and kept waving. The robots waved back at us, even as we shot off into the sky. For a long time they stood there waving. And it seemed to me I could see Ann Two and Jeff waving even after the others had gone below the surface.

Danny thought so too.

And then Dad headed for home and C.O.L.A.R. disappeared.

16

EVERY END IS A NEW BEGINNING

Our story should end here, but it doesn't. Because every end is really a new beginning.

When we got back to Earth, Mom went to her PTA meetings and I started school again and Danny waited for me after school and we'd walk home and talk about it. About C.O.L.A.R. It was something we couldn't get out of our minds.

We would be climbing trees or fishing and think about it.

Or after playing basketball, we'd remember C.O.L.A.R.

We just couldn't get it out of our minds.

Then one night while he was getting his battery charge and I was having a hard time falling asleep, I decided the time had come to confront C.O.L.A.R. again . . . and the unfinished business we had there.

"Danny."

"Yes, Jack."

"We said we were going to try to help the robots of C.O.L.A.R. live on the surface and see real sunlight and real trees, didn't we?"

"Yes," Danny said.

"How are we going to help them if we don't tell someone about C.O.L.A.R. and try to get people to understand?"

It was a good question and Danny had been worrying about it too.

"I think, Jack," he said slowly, "we're going to have to take a chance."

"I think so too."

It would be a big risk telling people about C.O.L.A.R. Maybe we had no right to do it. Yet something was making us want to do it.

The next evening at the supper table I told Mom and Dad what we had decided to do.

They agreed that while it was risky, it was worth a try. Especially if we didn't tell people where C.O.L.A.R. was.

Dad felt we ought to begin with Dr. Atkins himself. He was one of the most important men in the world. He had the ear of presidents and generals. And if he was understanding, then maybe C.O.L.A.R. could get established as a country and the robots wouldn't have to live underground.

Mom and Dad and me and Danny made an appointment and we went to see Dr. Atkins at his factory.

Dr. Atkins looked a little grayer than when we had first gone to his factory to get Danny, but he looked just as clever and important, and he regarded us with those same intelligent blue eyes that he had designed for Jeff.

"Go ahead, Jack," Dad said to me, "tell him everything."

Hoping he would understand, that he wouldn't get angry, I told him what had happened to the four of us that day we ran out of fuel in space.

Dr. Atkins sat and listened. When I was done he made Danny and me describe the passageways, the rooms, the Earthroom especially, and then he made us twice describe C.O.L.A.R. Control.

It was then that he asked us to draw the map you see on page 86.

He studied that map carefully. You could

see he was going over and over in his mind the things we told him. Danny and I looked at each other worried. It was occurring to us (a little late) that even though Dr. Atkins didn't know exactly where C.O.L.A.R. was (we hadn't told him), he could easily find out by checking the Space Patrol files for the location of a fuel transfer from them to the Jameson family spaceship.

Having found that out, he could quickly order police and soldiers into rocketships and send them to destroy C.O.L.A.R., capture the robots, and return them to their owners.

What a crazy thing Danny and I had just done. We'd risked the destruction of Ann Two, and all the robot boys and girls.

Fortunately, Dr. Atkins reacted differently.

"You know," he said quietly, "I have created better than I knew. I made robots brighter in many cases than human beings, and they, in turn, created a world for themselves.

"My dear Jameson family, the four of you did right to take a chance and tell me about C.O.L.A.R. I won't let it be destroyed. It is, indeed, my finest creation, and I intend to see that it survives and thrives—

"I'll pay back the owners of Atkins's Robots who have run away to live there. And I shall start an educational program for all people who want to buy robots. I'll make certain that Atkins's Robots are never mistreated again.

"And finally, I'll make certain that C.O.L.A.R. is recognized by all governments in the universe as a land where Atkins's Robots are living and—" his blue eyes twinkled, "playing."

"Bless you," Mom said.

And we all agreed to that.

Dr. Atkins was as good as his word. He contacted all the owners of runaway robots and paid them back their money. He set up educational programs for all present and future robot owners. And then, after we told him exactly where C.O.L.A.R. was, he contacted the heads of governments and all the Space Patrols and made sure everyone knew that C.O.L.A.R. was an independent planet and should be treated with respect.

After that it remained only to get word of these exciting happenings to Jeff, Ann Two, and the other robots.

Dr. Atkins said he'd radio them.

Danny and I begged to be permitted to take this exciting news to the robots ourselves. A radio message could scare them. They might not even believe it.

But if we went ourselves . . . (and brought a special present from him and us) . . .

Mom and Dad were willing. Danny and I would hire a space taxi. Dr. Atkins said it was all right with him. After what we had gone through, we deserved to be bearers of good news.

So that Christmas, when school let out, Danny and I flew in a space taxi from New Jersey to C.O.L.A.R. The pilot was pretty dubious about the whole thing, especially when we told him to set down in a crater on a small, airless-looking planet.

"You sure you want to land there?" he asked.

"Positive," I said.

"And keep the motor running," Danny said. "We probably won't be there long."

The pilot shook his head, but he did as we asked.

In fact, we had picked out the same crater that our family ship had landed in a couple of months earlier.

"I hope you boys know what you're doing," the taxi pilot said.

The clusters of rocks were to the rear. He wouldn't see a thing, which would be good. There's never any point in flustering a taxi pilot.

Danny and I got out slowly, because we were carrying between us a rather long and heavy box.

C.O.L.A.R.'s surface looked exactly the same—desolate, unfriendly, and pitted with craters. A slight wind whipped dust around our shoes and ankles.

We set the box down and waited.

The rocks were there, but not the five elevator rocks. Unless something had gone wrong below, we could expect to see five rocks rising, and then all over the land, metal covers popping off, and robot boys and girls climbing out.

We waited. Danny grinned nervously. "They sure got here faster last time."

"They have to be more careful now. They might think we betrayed them. And this is a different ship than ours."

Danny grabbed my arm. "Here they come."

My heart started pounding with excitement.

And happiness. They were okay. They were coming up. Slowly the five rocks rose from the land, and beyond them, we could see little heads emerging from the emergency ladders. . . .

And then the rocks reached full height and stopped.

Beyond them, robots appeared carrying shovels. Danny and I grinned at each other. This time they would really use those shovels.

Out of the rocks came Jeff, and Ann Two and Carl Three . . . and two more robots.

Ann Two and Jeff ran to us. All the other robots began running toward us too.

"Jack and Danny," Ann Two yelled, "you came back. The way you said you would."

Jeff was wary. "Why have you come back?" he asked.

"We wanted to bring you something," Danny said gravely. He pointed to the box.

"What is it?" Jeff asked, looking even more worried.

Now all the robot boys and girls were gathered in a circle around us and they were looking curiously at the box Danny and I had brought all the way from Earth.

"Open it," I said.

The robots looked at one another.

Then Ann Two said: "I'll open it."

She was always one to take a chance.

"Stand back everyone," Jeff warned.

He was thinking it could be a destruction machine of some kind.

The robots stepped backward.

Ann Two untied the string . . . and then opened the box. She stared at what was inside. And then she began to cry. But they were tears of happiness.

"What is it?" Jeff said.

The others now came crowding around.

"What's in there?" they asked.

Ann Two took our gift out of the box and held it up in the air for them all to see: a little live tree ready to be planted on C.O.L.A.R.'s surface.

They all stared at it.

"What does this mean?" Jeff asked.

"It means you can live free on the surface," I said.

"It's a present from us and Dr. Atkins," Danny said.

And then in a joyful tumble of words we

told them what had happened on Earth and how Dr. Atkins had made it possible for C.O.L.A.R. to function as a free and independent planet.

The robots looked at one another. They wanted to believe what they had just heard, but they were afraid to. It was almost too good to be true.

Finally Ann Two, still holding the seedling tree, said to me: "Danny, is it true?"

"I'm Jack," I said, "and it's true."

She turned to Danny.

"Danny," she said, "is it true?"

"It's true, Ann Two," Danny said.

Tears were rolling down Ann Two's cheeks. She turned to the others. "We're free at last," she cried. "Long live C.O.L.A.R."

"Long live C.O.L.A.R.," they shouted.

Jeff frowned. "Come on, everyone, don't just stand around. You've got shovels with you. Let's plant this tree before it dies. Someone get some water—"

A boss is always a boss.

Everyone wanted to have a hand in planting the tree, and just about everyone of them did.

After that it was time for Danny and me to go.

Nobody got too sad about our leaving, because we promised to return for lots of visits. Besides, our last view of C.O.L.A.R. as we shot upward into the sky was of a hundred robot boys and girls sitting around their new little tree.

"I bet when we come back there'll be a forest there," Danny said.

"I hope so, Jack," I said.

"Hey, wait a second," Danny said. "I'm Danny and you're Jack."

"Are you sure?"

"Hmm—" he said, and, laughing, we sped home.

*Eighty-two tricks you **can't** do!*

Science Impossibilities to Fool You

by Vicki Cobb and Kathy Darling
illus. by Martha Weston

Bet you can't tear a piece of paper into three equal
parts, or make two pencil tips meet. Bet you can't
blow up a balloon in a bottle. Bet you can't keep a
match burning over a glass of soda. Here are over
seventy deceptively simple—and impossible—
feats to stump friends and family while introducing
the scientific principles of gravity, mechanics,
logic, and perception. Winner of the Academy of
Science Children's Book Award.

Avon Camelot   54502-0 • $1.95

Also by Vicki Cobb and Kathy Darling
BET YOU CAN! *Science Possibilities to Fool You*
82180-X • $1.95

BOOK ONE

Sir Arthur Conan Doyle's
THE ADVENTURES OF
SHERLOCK HOLMES

Adapted for young readers by Catherine Edwards Sadler

Whose footsteps are those on the stairs of 221-B Baker Street, home of Mr. Sherlock Holmes, the world's greatest detective? And what incredible mysteries will challenge the wits of the genius sleuth this time?

A Study In Scarlet In the first Sherlock Holmes story ever written, Holmes and Watson embark on their first case together—an intriguing murder mystery.
The Red-headed League Holmes comes to the rescue in a most unusual heist!
The Man With The Twisted Lip Is this a case of murder, kidnapping, or something totally unexpected?

Join the uncanny and extraordinary Sherlock Holmes, and his friend and chronicler, Dr. Watson as they tackle dangerous crimes and untangle the most intricate mysteries.

AVON CAMELOT

WAYNE GRETZKY:
Portrait of a Hockey Player

by Craig Thomas Wolff

*black-and-white photographs
throughout by Bruce Curtis*

Here is the amazing personal and career life story
of one of the greatest ice hockey players ever.
Taught to play hockey by his father in his back yard,
Wayne Gretzky signed his professional contract
with the Edmonton Oilers at the age of seventeen,
and went on to shatter every major record in the
National Hockey League. Learn the fundamentals
of hockey and receive advice from Wayne Gretzky
on how to play ice hockey, one of the fastest growing and exhilirating sports today.

Avon Camelot Original   82420-5 • $1.95